An Old School Tie

ALSO BY ANDREW TAYLOR

An Old School Tie

A Novel of Suspense

Andrew Taylor

Dodd, Mead & Company

New York

Published by Dodd, Mead & Company, Inc.
79 Madison Avenue, New York, N.Y. 10016
Manufactured in the United States of America

First published in 1986 by Victor Gollancz Ltd., London

Library of Congress Cataloging-in-Publication Data

Taylor, Andrew, 1951–
An old school tie.

I. Title.
PR6070.A79056   1986   823'.914   86-11499
ISBN 0-396-08878-3

For Irene

An Old School Tie

One

William Dougal said the first thing which came into his head: "The last time I saw your name in *The Times*, it was in the obituary column."

"Times change, my dear William. And we must change with them."

James Hanbury picked up the newspaper and read the relevant entry aloud, perhaps because he feared that Dougal might have missed something in his excitement.

" 'The engagement is announced between James, the son of Mr. C. E. Hanbury, of Gloucester, and the late Mrs. Hanbury, and Mary, daughter of the late Colonel A. J. and the late Mrs. Margaret Burnham, of the Dower House, Charleston Parva, Cambridgeshire.' It sounds very well, you must admit. Molly will be sending you an invitation, of course."

"I don't think I'll be able to come."

"Why ever not?"

Dougal shrugged. "It would be unwise."

"No one would recognize you. It's over two years since you went to Rosington."

"But it must be the same Molly Burnham. The one with Sophie."

"I call her Oaf—Sophie, I mean. I've never liked fox terriers, and she's a remarkably ugly specimen of the breed, both physically and spiritually. Molly's short-sighted—of course she won't remember you."

Before Dougal could raise another objection, the older man adroitly changed the subject. There was plenty to talk about, since they had not seen one another for nearly two years. Dougal had hoped this desirable state of affairs might last for ever; but Hanbury had dashed the hope by turning up on his front doorstep with two bottles of malt whisky. It would have been churlish to turn away such a house-warming present. Besides, before Dougal had time to make up his mind, Hanbury was already in the tiny hall.

The obvious topic of conversation was Dougal's new flat. Until three weeks ago, Dougal had rented a converted billiards room in a decaying mansion in West Hampstead. Now he was the owner-occupier of a first-floor flat in a terrace house in Kilburn. In geographical terms, he had moved about a mile westwards; the social distance was considerably further. In Kilburn, you saw life in the raw; in West Hampstead, it usually wore its best clothes.

Hanbury insisted on taking a guided tour of the flat. This did not take very long because, apart from the kitchen and the bathroom, there were only two rooms; and neither of them contained much furniture. He winced when he saw the bedroom, which had nothing but a trunk, a double-mattress and two tins of white paint on its bare floorboards.

"*Décor minceur*, as it were." He picked up the photograph on the trunk. "Is this the latest? Nice bone structure. You must bring her to the wedding."

"I doubt it." Dougal had no intention of introducing Celia to Hanbury. Moreover, as far as he was aware, Celia had no desire to be taken anywhere by him. He took the photograph from Hanbury and restored it to the trunk.

They returned to the living room. Hanbury, perhaps sensing that he had been treading on dangerous ground, hastened to introduce another subject. He nodded towards the table by the window; on it were three box files, a pile of library books and a typewriter.

"Have you gone back to university? I seem to remember you were doing an M. Phil. when we first met. I always thought it was a pity you didn't finish it."

A snort of laughter escaped Dougal. One reason why he had not completed the M. Phil. was that Hanbury had garrotted his tutor. He turned the laugh into a cough and offered Hanbury some more of the whisky he had brought.

"It's not exactly academic work. I do freelance research these days. It earns a modest living."

"Dear me," said Hanbury. "How enterprising of you." He sounded faintly puzzled, as if the concepts of modesty and earning a living were equally foreign to him. "Don't tell me you've got a mortgage as well?"

Dougal, whose present existence was haunted by the monthly repayment to his bank, ignored this remark. "I had no idea how exciting being a home-owner is. I've acquired a completely different set of interests. Last night I dreamed about buying a door mat. The night before it was window-boxes; I thought I might grow some herbs."

"I'm rather looking forward to being a householder myself. Molly and I will live at the Dower House, of course. I believe you know it?"

"Only very slightly." Dougal had been there only once, as Hanbury knew very well. Since a murderer had been among his fellow guests, it was not an occasion he cared to remember.

"Old Mrs. Burnham died last autumn. Quite senile, of course. She left everything to Molly, which was only

3

right and proper. The house is in a terrible state of repair, but at least the money's available to do it up."

"How did you come to know Molly?" The question had been puzzling Dougal ever since he had read the news of the engagement.

"Oh, I've known her for years. Have I never mentioned I was at school in Rosington? The Burnhams have always had a strong connection with the school."

"A long courtship with a happy ending?"

Hanbury began to frown but thought better of it. "Now don't be cynical, William. The fact that Molly's now a wealthy woman has got nothing to do with this. Well, perhaps a little: but not much. I really want to settle down. I've had enough of living on my—ah—wits. I want my own fireside and a place in the community. I've reached my climacteric, as it were. The time has come to follow your example and become a solid citizen."

"I wish you luck." Dougal drained his glass and glanced at his watch.

Hanbury took the hint. "I must be off. Molly and I are dining with some extremely stuffy cousins of hers tonight, and I shall almost certainly be late. Besides, I've kept my taxi waiting for the last half-hour."

He picked up his umbrella and led the way into the hall. He glanced at his reflection in the mirror which Dougal had hung there in an attempt to create an illusion of spaciousness. His dark-blue suit was in his usual restrained taste; but the silk tie, which consisted of alternating stripes of pink and silver, added an uncharacteristically garish touch. Hanbury straightened it. His eyes met Dougal's in the mirror.

"Rather lurid, isn't it? But tactful—it's an Old Rosingtonian tie. Molly likes me to wear it."

Dougal opened the door. "Thanks for the whisky."

"You will come to the wedding, won't you? My side

of the church is going to be very sparsely populated compared with Molly's. The trouble is, most of my acquaintances aren't the sort of people you want at your wedding."

Dougal hardened his heart against the note of pleading in Hanbury's voice. "I'm sorry, James. There's an outside chance that someone might recognize me—and might remember I had a different name the last time I was in Rosington."

"Think it over. Just for me." Hanbury glanced at the head of the stairs which led to the communal front door. "You could always grow a beard. You're halfway there already."

Dougal fingered the stubble on his chin and shook his head. "Beards itch."

"I would be happy to defray your expenses."

"Isn't that your taxi hooting outside?"

One Saturday nearly five weeks later, Dougal found himself in the cloister garth of Rosington Cathedral. He wore his father's morning coat and carried a top hat which was a size too small to wear on his head. The weather was unseasonably fine for an English June, as if God wished to emphasize that the newly wedded couple enjoyed his entire approval. A perspiring photographer was trying to persuade the guests to stand still for a moment.

The organ thundered faintly inside the cathedral. By a special dispensation of the Dean and Chapter, the new Mrs. Hanbury's dogs had been allowed into the cloisters. David and Benji, the Airedales, had been infected by the decorum of the occasion. They sat gravely on guard a few feet away from Mr. and Mrs. Hanbury, and allowed the younger guests to pat them respectfully on their massive heads.

The third dog, Sophie, was less constrained by her surroundings. She trundled round the little garden, as ineluctable as Fate, obeying some obscure canine imperative of her own. This imperative led her to urinate on the tombstones of two minor canons and to nip the photographer on the ankle.

Her mistress called her, but to no avail. "It's the heat," she explained to her husband. "The poor thing doesn't know what she's doing."

"Rubbish!" said a voice on the level of Dougal's elbow. "It's bad temper. That dog should be put down."

A wizened man with a shock of white hair was sitting in a wheelchair just behind him. A uniformed nurse was several yards away with her back to them; she was talking to the school chaplain who had helped the dean conduct the service.

The old man glanced behind him to make sure she was still engaged. A gnarled hand shot out and gripped Dougal's.

"Hanbury. Groom's father. Got a drink? Or a cigarette? She's not looking, is she?"

Dougal shook his head. He was in the middle of giving up smoking for the third time this year; he wasn't in the habit of carrying a flask around with him; and the nurse, six feet tall and broad to match, was tittering at something the chaplain had said.

"I hate weddings," the elder Hanbury confided in a whisper which echoed round the cloisters. "You drive all the way from Gloucester, then you sit for hours in a damned draught church; you hang around while other people play with their cameras; and then if you're lucky you get a mouthful of bubbles. Pa! I'm damned if I'll let that stupid woman rot my insides with tea."

Hanbury glanced round, noted that he was attracting attention, and changed his piercing whisper to a quavering shriek. "Sunnyvale! That's where me and that woman live. I call it the vale of tears."

6

The nurse returned in a hurry to discipline her charge and Dougal wandered away. The wedding was proving much less of an ordeal than he had expected. He recognized only two people apart from Hanbury—the bride and the best man, Sir Thomas Graver. Neither of them had known him well. In any case his new beard, scruffy though it was, camouflaged his face with surprising efficiency; when he caught sight of his own reflection, it seemed to belong to someone else.

He moved through the crowd, eavesdropping on conversations and trying to categorize the other guests. He was still a little uncertain why he was here. It was true that Hanbury had characteristically refused to take no for an answer: the wedding invitation had duly arrived, accompanied by a first-class return by British Rail from London to Rosington. There was also a note to the effect that Dougal needn't bother with a wedding present since Hanbury had already bought it for him.

But curiosity had been a stronger motive for coming. It was almost impossible to envisage a domesticated and respectable Hanbury; it was necessary to see the transformation in the flesh.

For Hanbury occupied a peculiar, almost mythological position in Dougal's memory. It was he who had pitchforked Dougal into two distinctly dubious enterprises, several years ago. The well-bred and impeccably dressed exterior was misleading: Hanbury was a broker of crime—or at least had been until his marriage. On one occasion he had appeared to die; but the report of his death, though published in both *The Times* and the *Daily Telegraph*, had proved premature.

In one way, Hanbury had done Dougal a favour: he had given him the best of reasons for trying to be a sober and law-abiding citizen. It followed that Hanbury's own metamorphosis into apparent respectability was a bizarre

7

and fascinating event. Dougal felt rather as he imagined a lapsed catholic would, on the news that the Pope had embraced atheism.

In a word, he felt oddly cheated.

"No sign of Jonathan Stride, I notice," said a gaunt, middle-aged woman beside him.

At first Dougal thought she was talking to him. But a short, dumpy lady, approaching across the close-cut grass, swiftly disabused him.

"I should think not. He's got more sense. Look at James Hanbury. As bold as brass! And still with that dreadful smirk on his face."

"Molly Burnham is going to regret this. You mark my words, Miss Carrot." The gaunt lady inched closer to her friend. "It won't last."

The two women were now so close together that their conversation became inaudible, to Dougal's great regret. He had already divided the guests into five tentative groups. These ladies, he guessed, belonged to the genteel substratum which developed in the shadow of the clergy in any small cathedral city. In the other categories were the clergy themselves; the people connected with Rosington School and its linked foundation, the Choir School; the people with booming voices and weather-beaten faces from the Fenlands around Rosington; and, finally and least cohesively, the group of strangers from the groom's side of the cathedral choir which included Sir Thomas Graver, the elder Mr. Hanbury and himself.

Dougal was forced to step backwards sharply to avoid a small girl who was sprinting towards the door to the south side of the cloisters. The girl's face was pink with terror, making it much the same colour as her sash, half of which trailed behind her. Sophie, the other half of the sash firmly clamped between her jaws waddled purposefully after her. She was followed in turn by the bride and by an agitated young couple who were presumably the little girl's parents.

In his haste to move back out of harm's—and specifically Sophie's—way, Dougal trod on a foot belonging to an old gentleman.

The man brushed aside his apologies. "No harm done." He nodded towards the scrimmage which had developed by the door to the south walk of the cloister. " 'The unspeakable in full pursuit of the uneatable,' as dear Oscar would have said. Ah! I see Molly is restraining Sophie. In some ways that is rather a pity. That pink was really a great mistake. Have you noticed how it clashes with the red carnations?"

Dougal observed that a white carnation was always a much wiser choice. It seemed a safe thing to say, since it implied that both he and the old gentleman were wise.

"How true. If you look around you here, you won't see any of *my* boys wearing a red carnation. Oh no! Grandpa's trained them—and that training lasts for life."

For a delightful instant Dougal wondered if every male with a white carnation present among the guests was a grandson of the old gentleman; there must have been at least fifty of them.

"But we have not been introduced. My name is Pantry—Evelyn Pantry."

Dougal mentioned his own name and they shook hands solemnly—and for rather longer than Dougal thought customary.

Pantry relinquished his hand with a sigh. "*Such* a lovely day for the wedding. You must be one of James's London friends." The pale-blue eyes behind the thick glasses were hard with curiosity.

"In a manner of speaking," Dougal admitted. "Have you known James for long?"

"Since he was thirteen. Best head of house I ever had.

9

I've known Molly since she was a girl as well. Dear me, yes! I remember old Colonel Burnham saying to me: 'I wish she was a boy, Evie: I could give her to you to lick into shape.' "

"I must confess I'm a little confused: there seem to be two schools."

"Ah yes, many outsiders find it difficult to grasp. The original foundation is the Choir School—that goes back to the Middle Ages. Then Henry VIII founded a grammar school, which eventually turned into the public school we are today. The Choir School is still in the cathedral precincts and serves in a sense as a prep school for Rosington School. Rosington itself was moved to a site outside the city in the last century. You follow me?"

"More or less. And James was at Rosington School?"

"Yes—but he was also at the Choir School beforehand. He had a lovely voice as a boy—quite angelic. And that's why he could be married in the cathedral. Ex-choristers have that privilege."

"Are you still at the school?"

"Alas no. 'His golden locks time hath to silver turned,' and so forth. They've put the old horse out to grass. Not that I don't canter around the paddock for them occasionally." Mr. Pantry looked faintly bemused, as if his metaphor had got out of control. "I still do a great deal of honorary work," he explained *en clair*. "Grandpa's retirement is more notional than actual. Still, one has a certain obligation—Ah! I think James needs me for the photographs. You'll excuse me, I'm sure."

Mr. Pantry set off across the lawn, walking with a remarkably spry step. The photographer had just succeeded in marshalling the protagonists of the event into the recess between two of the buttresses of the north wall of the cloister. Hanbury, top hat in hand, looked large, magnificent and protective. Molly, her grey hair askew and her square face alight with joy, was hanging on his arm and staring up at his face. She was flanked by Leo Cumblesham, a benign old man, strongly resembling a grizzly bear, who had given her away; beyond him was the matron of honour, who belonged without a doubt to the booming-voice-and-weatherbeaten-face brigade. Next to Hanbury was Sir Thomas, who was staring unhappily at the ground, and Mr. Hanbury Senior who was apparently asleep.

"Here I am, James!" Pantry slid between Sir Thomas and the wheelchair. "Now, my man," he said to the photographer, "I suggest you use the buttresses and the arch of the window behind us to frame your photograph." He turned to Sir Thomas. "I remember dear Cecil saying—Cecil Beaton, that is—"

A howl of rage drowned Mr. Pantry's voice and silenced the murmur of chatter in the cloister garth. Everyone, Dougal included, had been looking in the direction of the photographer and his subjects. Now, with one accord, they swung round.

A short, pear-shaped man in his early thirties was framed in the south doorway. He had long black hair, already receding at the temples; he wore a torn T-shirt and faded black jeans; his bare feet were much the same colour as his jeans.

"Look at you," he screamed. He arched back his arm and threw something red and round, for all the world like a fielder aiming at a wicket. The crowd parted beneath its path like the Red Sea. Every face was upturned and frozen with shock.

Sophie gave two short, sharp barks.

The missile was aimed directly at Mr. and Mrs. Hanbury; it was impossible to tell whether one or both of them was the target. Molly's face was blank with horror. She was clinging to her husband's arm. With his free hand, Hanbury doffed his top hat.

The overripe tomato smacked on to the crown of the hat. Without this barrier, it would have hit the linked arms of the couple. The impetus of its flight pulped the fruit against the grey material which covered the hat. Juice spurted; red flesh and yellow seeds slid from the hat to the grass.

"Well played, sir!" screeched the elder Mr. Hanbury.

A number of the younger male guests converged on the intruder. Mr. Pantry scampered across the grass and directed operations from the rear. Sophie knocked over the photographer's tripod and slobbered over Molly's hand. The Airedales tried to pretend that nothing had happened.

A few yards away from Dougal, the rosy colour drained away from Miss Carrot's well-padded cheeks. She collapsed on the lawn in a huddle of turquoise chiffon.

Dougal and Hanbury collided as they rushed to help the stricken lady. For an instant as they disentangled themselves, their eyes met. Dougal glimpsed an unfamiliar expression on the older man's face. It was not until they were both kneeling beside Miss Carrot that he recognized the expression for what it was.

Hanbury was afraid.

Seven weeks later, towards the end of July, the name Hanbury reappeared in *The Times*.

Dougal noticed it quite by chance as he was skimming through the paper in the direction of the crossword. The name leapt out at him from the section of the Personal Columns which was devoted to memorial services. His immediate reaction was to assume that Hanbury's delinquent father had finally evaded his nursemaid.

HANBURY—A Service of Thanksgiving for the life of Mrs. Mary Elizabeth Hanbury, JP, will be held in Rosington Cathedral on Thursday, 25th July, at 12 noon.

Two

Hanbury had aged.

Usually he looked like a young forty; now he looked like an elderly fifty. He was waiting on the platform as the train drew in, his head bowed, jabbing the asphalt with the tip of his umbrella. There were more streaks of grey in his hair than there had been before; and the hair itself needed cutting. He did not look up as the train wheezed to a halt.

Dougal got out of the second-class smoker—his resolution had cracked again—and, bag in hand, walked up to his host.

"William," said Hanbury dully. "Good of you to come."

Dougal muttered something which began as "Not at all" and ended as "Only too glad" with an awkward hiatus of silence in the middle.

Hanbury's clothes lacked their usual dapper formality. He wore neither jacket nor tie; his shirt was grubby and frayed; and his trousers looked as if he had slept in them.

"I've got the car outside." He took Dougal's bag and led the way towards the barrier. "Yesterday went very well. We got the bishop."

"I'm sorry I couldn't come to the service."

Dougal privately wished that he had been sufficiently ruthless to refuse Hanbury's invitation for the weekend instead. But he had found it impossible to resist the misery in Hanbury's voice over the telephone last night: *For God's sake, William, you must come. I shall go mad if I spend another night alone in this house.*

The tarmac on the station forecourt glistened with rain. As Hanbury put up the umbrella there was a flash of lightning, followed by a long roll of thunder directly overhead. Dougal glanced up the hill at the cathedral, half a mile away. It dwarfed the roofs of the town which clustered around its protective bulk. It was like a great stone insect, squatting on the haunches of its west towers; the octagonal central spire was a proboscis which stabbed the firmament.

"The car's over there," Hanbury said, pointing towards a Range Rover from which a muffled chorus of barking could be heard. "I had to bring the dogs. They keep thinking I'm going to take them for a walk."

A taxi drew up, spraying muddy water on Hanbury's trousers. A dumpy lady, whom Dougal recognized as Miss Carrot, got out and hurried into the station. Hanbury half bowed and started to say something; but she cut him dead.

There was little chance of conversation on the seven-mile drive to Charleston Parva. The two Airedales had compressed themselves into the smallest possible area; they crouched in the corner, between the side window and the metal grill which divided the rear of the Range Rover from the front, alternately whining and yapping. Sophie confronted them, her legs planted widely apart, barking monotonously and piercingly.

Hanbury said: "I don't think that bloody dog has stopped barking since Molly died." He had to repeat it twice before Dougal could catch what he was saying.

The rain beat against the windscreen, and the wipers slapped to and fro, adding to the noise. Their route took them across the Fens by a series of B-roads which zig-zagged, often on embankments, above the limitless sea of mud. It looked as if the Fens were doing their best to return to their primeval waterlogged state.

There was little traffic on the roads, which was just as well because Hanbury's driving was reckless. For most of the journey the roads were straight as a surveyor could make them, and Hanbury pushed the Range Rover up to a steady 90 m.p.h. This led to problems when the zigs became zags, and vice versa, for many of the bends were unexpectedly acute. There was one particularly nasty moment when they rounded a corner on the wrong side of the road and found themselves confronting a tractor.

Hanbury swerved, stamping on the brakes. Rubber squealed and the Range Rover buried its nose in the embankment on the far side of the road. Dougal jerked forward against his seatbelt. There was a mighty clatter as Sophie collided with the grill. She was so surprised that for a few seconds she forgot to bark.

The tractor driver, a black-browed woman with a headscarf, shook her fist and upbraided them in a broad and incomprehensible Fen accent. Hanbury rolled down his window and stuck out his head.

"You're a bloody boggo, ma'am," he snarled. "You should keep off the roads and stay in the mud where you belong."

He engaged four-wheel drive and roared off, spraying the tractor with mud. Dougal prayed silently to St. Christopher. It was not just Hanbury's driving which terrified him: it was the change in his temperament. Usually Hanbury was urbane to a fault; this boorish savagery was wholly unexpected.

The road rose as, to Dougal's relief, they reached the rocky outcrop on which Charleston Parva, like most Fen villages, was built. The hamlet clustered round a crossroads. Each of the principal buildings—the Parish Church of St. Tumwulf, the pub, the village shop and the Dower House—was tucked into one corner of the crossroads. Beyond the village shop was a row of studiously unpicturesque cottages built of dirty yellow brick.

They turned left, between the Dower House and the Burnham Arms, and left again into a courtyard behind the house. Hanbury drove straight into what had once been a coach-house.

Once released from their confinement, the dogs rushed through an archway which connected the courtyard with the garden at the side of the house. Dougal and Hanbury followed, sheltering under the umbrella. The dogs bounded across the overgrown lawn and plunged into a dank and luxuriant shrubbery.

Hanbury sighed with relief. "We'll get a few minutes peace, with luck."

He led Dougal down a gravel path, parallel with the side of the house, to a pair of french windows. The windows, which were unlocked, gave on to a large, square sitting room whose panelled walls had once been painted white.

"I know it's early, but I could do with a drink."

Hanbury crossed the room, leaving a trail of damp footprints on the faded grey carpet, to a sideboard on the left of the door. The decanter had only an inch of whisky in it. He brought out a fresh bottle and carried both, one in each hand, to the low circular table in front of the empty fireplace.

"Not for me, thanks." Dougal closed the windows. There was already a puddle on the carpet. The rain beat against the panes, blurring the garden beyond. "It seems later than it is, doesn't it? The storm makes everything so dark."

Hanbury sat down heavily in the armchair near the table. He emptied the decanter into a glass which was already waiting for him.

"You don't have to make drawing room conversation, you know."

Dougal moved away from the window. In the gloom he stumbled against the edge of the carpet. "Shall I turn on a light?"

To the right of the fireplace was a standard lamp with an immense tasselled shade of orange silk. He stretched out his hand towards it.

"No—don't do that." Hanbury's drink slopped in his hand. He took another mouthful of it. "I—ah—I'm not using the electricity at present."

Dougal sat down opposite his host. "Why not?"

"Molly was electrocuted in this house." Hanbury reached for the unopened bottle. "And everyone except the coroner—"

Three loud knocks boomed through the house.

The knocks were equally spaced in a slow rhythm. Each one sounded as if it would raise the dust in the attics. They were knocks with a sense of their own importance.

Hanbury's lassitude vanished abruptly. By the second knock he was on his feet; by the third he was at one of the windows which gave on to the front of the house.

"Can't see a thing," he muttered. "That damned Virginia creeper is in the way."

He straightened his shoulders and left the room, one hand smoothing his hair. Dougal followed him into the hall which lay beyond. To the left, at the back of the hall, a broad staircase with shallow treads rose to the upper floors, bifurcating at the mezzanine level. Opposite it was the front door, surmounted by a half-oval fanlight which was obscured by grime and Virginia creeper.

Hanbury opened the door and a gust of air swept into the house. On the doorstep was a woman with a red face, seamed with lines. The eyes and the mouth were compressed into parallel slits. Her hair was tightly permed against her small skull; and her body was rendered shapeless by the slate-coloured mackintosh she wore. Above her head was an umbrella, from whose perimeter ran countless rivulets of rain. As she opened her mouth to speak, there was a roll of thunder. To Dougal it seemed as though the heavens were speaking through her lips.

"*There* you are, Mrs. Palmer." Hanbury made it sound as if he had been single-mindedly scouring Charleston Parva for her. "Do come in. I wanted to ask your advice about the Aga. It—"

"I've come for my money," Mrs. Palmer announced, ignoring Hanbury's words entirely. "Up to the end of last week, if you please."

"Of course." Hanbury pulled out a roll of notes from his trouser pocket, peeled off half a dozen of them and held them out.

The speed with which she snatched them suggested not greed, but that the hand from which they came was hot, and that the notes themselves were conductors of heat. As she took them her body, and hence the umbrella above it, inclined forward. A gout of rainwater spurted on to Hanbury's outstretched arm.

"I've been thinking, Mrs. Palmer: we really should discuss your—ah—salary. It seems to me you're long overdue for a rise. I know Molly would have—"

"I'll just take what's owed to me, Mr. Hanbury." One

of the notes slipped through her fingers and fluttered on to the threshold. "I meant what I said last week. You'll just have to find someone else."

Hanbury closed the door so gently that he must have been resisting the temptation to slam it. He turned to face Dougal, his shoulders slumped.

"That was the daily. She's been charring here for thirty years. Molly inherited her with the house."

"It sounds like she's given you the sack."

"Typical Fen mentality—believe all possible evil. For two pins the locals would burn me at the stake."

Dougal followed Hanbury back into the sitting room. "James, why don't you tell me what all this is about?"

Hanbury picked up his glass. "The authorities are perfectly happy that Molly's death was a domestic accident. But everyone else seems to be convinced that I murdered her."

The uncomfortable silence was broken by the sound of a heavy body throwing itself repeatedly against the french windows. Hanbury opened them, and the dogs streamed into the sitting room, with Sophie in the lead. The Airedales shook themselves vigorously and careered through the door to the hall. Sophie lumbered over to Dougal and sniffed suspiciously at his hand. She then turned through a hundred and eighty degrees and stretched, immodestly presenting her posterior to him. Once these rites were completed, she sat down heavily on his right foot.

"If I left the area, they'd say I was running away. If I put those damned dogs in kennels, they'd say I was callous. And if I had Sophie put down—and God knows, she's a four-legged argument for euthanasia—half the county would rise up in arms."

Sophie growled at him.

Dougal stirred in his chair. "How did it happen?"

"Molly's death? I'll show you. She died in the study."

Hanbury took him to a room on the other side of the hall. Its two windows were separated from the road by a strip of flowerbed and a row of black iron railings, topped with spikes in the shape of fleur-de-lis. The plaster on one of the external walls was streaked with damp. The furniture was dark and bulky. The cornices were grey with spiders' webs. On one wall was a large oak desk, flanked by glass-fronted bookcases which stretched high above Dougal's head. Dougal gained a fleeting impression of elderly reference books and rows of pre-war novels, still in their original jackets.

"No one's used the room since Molly's uncle died. Molly was going to do it up for me. She wanted me to have a *private* room, you see. She was very old-fashioned in some ways: I think she felt that men needed somewhere to smoke cigars and look at *Sporting Life*. It's ironic, really—she was so insistent about it being *my* room. Yet it was here she died."

Dougal shivered. A woman whom he had last seen in her wedding-dress had had the life fried out of her in this room.

"See that?" Hanbury pointed to an electric lamp on the desk. Its base was a brass candlestick, richly ornamented with cornucopias and lions' heads; it was about a foot high and looked solid enough to brain an elephant. It had a tulip-shaped shade which appeared to be made of cracked parchment.

"There used to be two of them. The candlesticks are probably mid-nineteenth century. They were converted into lamps at least fifty years ago, maybe longer."

Dougal bent down to examine it. The socket which held the bulb and switch was of brass; unlike its modern counterparts, it lacked an earth terminal. The flex, which ran down through the centre of the candlestick and emerged at the base, was partly covered with frayed fabric; in some places metal glinted through. He followed the flex down to the plug which lay unconnected on the carpet. Like the socket in the nearby skirting-board, it was one of the old-fashioned, round-pin variety; it would not have had a separate fuse.

"The house needed rewiring," Hanbury said helplessly. "It was one of the first things we were going to do." His voice hardened: "Mrs. Burnham was living in a deathtrap for years—and it killed Molly."

Dougal looked up. "Round-pin sockets mean radial wiring, don't they? Each socket has its own power supply—and its own fuse."

Hanbury nodded. "The fuse box is in the back hall. The police checked it, of course. You know the sort of thing; the fuses are bits of wire in porcelain holders; each bit of wire is meant to be the right number of amps for the appliance used. Or so they tell me."

"And this one wasn't?"

"The fuse must have blown years ago. Someone had replaced it with ordinary copper wire. It wouldn't have blown if you'd plugged a couple of cookers into it." His face crumpled and he added, in a voice so low that Dougal had to strain to catch the words: "Let alone a human being."

Embarrassment made Dougal ruthless. "It wasn't this lamp which—?"

Hanbury shook his head. "The police took it away, thank God. But that's its twin. The live wire was shorting on to the candlestick itself. As soon as Molly touched it, she earthed it."

Dougal extracted the rest of the story with a series of questions. It was a painful process—he felt like a surgeon extracting shrapnel from a wound; but, like a surgeon, he hoped he was causing pain in order ultimately to relieve it. Hanbury, he suspected, needed to talk—otherwise he would not have asked Dougal to stay.

The tragedy had happened on the day after they returned from their honeymoon in Sri Lanka. In the evening Hanbury went into Rosington, leaving Molly watching television in the sitting room. She must have gone into the study after darkness was fallen. The bulb in the overhead light had gone, so Molly must have reached for the lamp on the desk.

"Where were the dogs?" Dougal asked.

"Molly had shut them in the sitting room, which was fortunate or unfortunate, according to your viewpoint: they might have been killed as well."

"Could someone have tampered with the fuse and the lamp?"

Hanbury shrugged. "One can always tamper with *anything*," he remarked with a certain authority on these matters. "The wire in the fuse was old and grimy—it could have been there for years. The local electrician testified that he'd never been asked to look at the wiring here. Mrs. Palmer told the coroner that she'd sooner talk to the devil than look inside a fuse box. *I'd* never looked inside it—why should I? I'd only been here for twenty-four hours. As for the lamp, the flex was frayed and brittle. The electrician said it was a miracle it hadn't shorted before."

Dougal looked sharply at Hanbury, a suspicion forming in his mind. He shelved it for the moment. "If there was no evidence that it was anything but an accident, why are your neighbours so convinced it was murder?"

Hanbury postponed answering while he found his Caporals, offered them to Dougal and lit both cigarettes with a slim gold lighter. "Molly belongs in this part of the world. I'm an outsider. They naturally think the worst of me."

"Why?" Dougal demanded.

Hanbury seemed to have heard a different question. "The Burnhams have been here for nearly three hundred years. They helped to drain the Fens—and used to own a lot of them, as well. They had fingers in every bit of the pie: Molly's grandfather was a Bishop of Rosington; Mrs. Burnham's grandfather practically refounded the school single-handed; they've represented Rosington in Parliament—"

"But why don't they like you?"

"What I'm trying to say is that it's a terribly inbred society. Literally, as well as metaphorically—you still hear amazing tales of incest on the outlying farms. They close ranks against outsiders. I went to school here, but that's not enough: I'm still a foreigner." Hanbury flicked ash in the grate. "And of course Molly was a very rich woman."

"And now you're a rich man?"

Hanbury coughed modestly. "We made wills in each other's favour just before we married. She made a few bequests—to the RSPCA, the cathedral, the school and so on—but the bulk of what she inherited from her aunt comes to me."

Dougal was silent for a moment. From his own experience he knew that Hanbury had certainly been capable of murder in the past, though the general public of Rosington were presumably unaware of this fact. His sudden marriage to a plain, middle-aged spinster was out of character, unless one took her wealth into account.

On the other hand, Dougal could have sworn that Hanbury was being sincere when, that evening before his marriage, he had talked of reaching his climacteric and his need to settle down. Hanbury was a businessman, albeit one with unorthodox methods, not a psychopath. If he had married for money—which was perfectly possible—he would only have taken the risk of murder as a last resort. Hanbury was an ingenious man: he would have tried other, safer methods of parting Molly from her money; and it was difficult to believe that he could have exhausted these in a few weeks.

There was another point which might be construed in favour of Hanbury's innocence: if guilty, he could have no reason to invite, or rather beg, Dougal to stay.

Hanbury threw the end of his cigarette into the grate. "I didn't kill her, William," he said softly. He stared out of the window. By now it was twilight; the storm had subsided into drizzle. "That's what you're wondering, isn't it?"

"It was one possibility," Dougal admitted. He could see no purpose in lying.

"Why should I kill her? She wanted us to have everything in common. I can show you letters—you can talk to our solicitor—the bank manager. And besides—"

Hanbury broke off; he seemed to be studying the shifting silver networks of water on the windowpane. Suddenly he swung round. It was impossible to see his expression: the darkness flattered his face to a near-silhouette.

"Besides, William, I—ah—loved her. Not at first, you understand. It developed almost without my noticing it. The pretence became the reality." Suddenly he smashed his fist into the wall, and his voice rose to a shout: *"It's all so bloody ironic."*

"All right, James, all right. What do you want me to do?"

Hanbury turned back to the window, supporting himself against the frame as if his outburst had exhausted his reserves of energy. "You're good at finding things out. You've got the nose for it, or the academic training, or whatever it is. You're a freelance researcher, so presumably I can hire you? I want you to find out whether or not Molly's death was an accident."

Dougal chose his words with care: "You've considered the third possibility?"

"What do you mean?" Hanbury sounded as if his nose was blocked.

"If it was murder, it's possible that Molly wasn't the intended victim. After all, you might have been the first to switch on that light."

Three

Dougal might have been hired as a researcher, but for the next few hours his duties combined those of a nursemaid and a housekeeper.

For the last week Hanbury had apparently been living on an exclusive diet of cold baked beans, sliced bread and whisky. Dougal started in the kitchen: it took him an hour to persuade the Ago to stay alight and to reduce the room to some semblance of order. He then cooked high tea—a curious but warming meal of tinned pheasant soup, scrambled eggs and overripe Stilton. They ate in the kitchen by the light of candles. By the time they had finished the water was hot enough for Hanbury to have a bath and a shave.

Dougal, meanwhile, washed up and fed the dogs. Hanbury was still splashing in the bathroom, so Dougal turned his attention to the beds. He found sheets and pillowcases, worn but meticulously clean, stacked in a linen cupboard on the first floor landing.

Hanbury's bedroom overlooked the garden. It was a large, airy room with a double-bed. Molly's brushes were still on the dressing-table, and her clothes hung in a wardrobe which smelled faintly and unpleasantly of Sophie.

Dougal changed the sheets and opened the window.

He made up a bed for himself in the smaller room next door. While he was working, Sophie followed him from room to room. Rather to Dougal's surprise, she made no attempt to impede him. In each room she sat by the door, staring at him with a cold and calculating eye. Sometimes she scratched the tumour—Hanbury had mentioned it while they were eating: "I regret to say it's benign"—which dangled from her belly.

Hanbury emerged from the bathroom as Dougal was unpacking his bag. He looked pink and scrubbed; his red silk dressing-gown and blue-and-white striped pyjamas gave him a festive air. He stumbled over Sophie. Molten wax from his candle dripped on to the carpet.

"I might have a nightcap before bed. Care to join me?"

Dougal nodded. He felt bone-weary: clearly he had neither the aptitude nor the training to make a success of domestic service. Hanbury led the way down to the sitting room. He poured the drinks while Dougal drew the curtains and lit more candles. The soft yellow light was kind to the room and to Hanbury: it concealed the shabbiness of the one and the haggardness of the other.

Hanbury sipped his whisky. "Have you had any ideas yet?"

"Not really. You realize that the odds are it was an accident? There's no evidence to the contrary."

"Perhaps. But I need to be sure—or at least as sure as it's possible to be. What avenues do you—ah—intend to pursue?"

"I thought I could go over the mechanics of it in the daylight—look at the fuse box, the wiring and the lamp. I doubt if there's anything to find—the police have been there first. But, if we assume it's murder, what about opportunity? Whoever did it would have needed access to the house; he or she would have needed to know about the wiring. Tinkering with the fuse and with that lamp would have taken some time. The whole business suggests a certain amount of premeditation."

"It's a big field." Hanbury yawned. "The Burnhams always did a lot of entertaining, even in the old lady's day. Scores of people would have known about the wiring. As for access, that wouldn't have been a problem: we were away for a month, and the house was empty. Mrs. Palmer came in once or twice a week, but that was all."

"Any sign of a break-in while you were away?"

Hanbury shook his head. "Not that it means anything. This place is about as secure as a shoe box. There's been a spare key to the back door on the kitchen windowsill for as long as anyone can remember."

"Were the dogs here?"

"No—in kennels."

Dougal lit a cigarette. "So it's likely that our hypothetical murderer had local knowledge."

In the silence which followed, another possibility occurred to Dougal which, if true, supported the theory that the murderer had local knowledge. Hanbury had undoubtedly made many enemies in his long and chequered career. But these would have been professionals. There was no reason why they should bother to set up a finicky and unreliable accident for him. They would have hired a contract killer who could do the job simply and efficiently with a bullet or a knife.

If there was a murderer, therefore, it was probable that it was an amateur who lived in the area.

He was aware that he was building an edifice of suppositions and possibilities; a single puff of reality could blow it away. He had no illusions about his job in the next few days. He was ostensibly investigating a murder which was probably nonexistent; but his real purpose was to try to prevent Hanbury from becoming an alcoholic recluse. For Hanbury's sake, though, he had to preserve appearances.

Hanbury refilled his glass and pushed the bottle across the table towards Dougal. His hand shook, and his eyes looked moist and glassy.

"It's the motive that puzzles me, William. It's inconceivable that it could have been gain. No one but myself benefited substantially from Molly's death. No one had any reason to hate her. It's true that some people in Rosington dislike *me*." Hanbury solemnly shook his head, as if this was a fact he was forced to recognize without understanding why it should be so. "But you don't try to kill someone because you dislike them, do you? It's most puzzling."

"I think it's time we went to bed." Dougal got to his feet and Hanbury shakily followed suit. "Is there anyone I could talk to? A fount of local gossip?"

"Ah." Hanbury picked up the whisky bottle and tucked it under his arm. "I know the very person."

For the last few seconds, a motorcycle had been approaching along the village street. The penetrating buzz of its engine had forced them both to raise their voices. Suddenly the buzz subsided.

Almost simultaneously, something crashed through the glass of the window nearest the front door. The curtains billowed into the room.

A half-brick thudded on to the carpet, the dogs began to bark. The motorbike raced away into the darkness.

"Dead baby."

Mr. Pantry gazed in triumph at his two guests, as if daring them to comment. He bent forward and poured a thin trickle of Lapsang Souchong into Dougal's cup.

"Dead baby," he explained, "was boiled baby injected

with red death. That's to say, steamed suet pudding to which a small quantity of raspberry-flavoured jam had been added. Dear me, yes: one could write volumes simply on the language. Some terms are obvious, of course. No one would be surprised to hear that chamber pots were called Burnham Cups, for example—the design of the House Rugger Cup is indeed strikingly similar to a potty's. But I fancy *Fug the scob* would puzzle most people."

"Oh, come on, Evelyn. Even I don't know what a scob is." Jonathan Stride dabbed a spot of tea from his Old Rosingtonian tie and grinned at Dougal. "I sometimes wonder if Evelyn makes up half the obsolete slang he pretends to discover."

"Really, Jon! As if Grandpa would do a thing like that! Scob had a relatively brief life in the nineteen-thirties. It was equivalent to 'cheat,' and could be used both as a noun and as a verb. It also meant a crib."

"And what about fug?" Dougal asked.

"A fug-box was a wastepaper basket. They were large and square and made of wood—still are, actually. Their name derived from their resemblance to the hampers for dirty washing, which naturally exuded a fug. To fug someone was to place his bottom (or *bim*), and as much of the rest of him as possible, in a fug-box."

Dougal laughed. Mr. Pantry chattered on about his projected monograph on the history of the school, with an appendix on its private language. The late afternoon sun slanted through the branches of the walnut tree at the end of the small walled garden. Yesterday's storm might never have existed: Saturday was doing its best to be a perfect summer day.

The tiny lawn was just large enough for three deck-chairs and the tea table. They had consumed China tea and cucumber sandwiches—made, as Mr. Pantry had been at pains to point out to them, with his own fair hands.

Dougal let the drone of his host's beautifully modulated voice wash over him like a soothing lotion. Hanbury's blend of grief and paranoia was immensely tiring: it was a relief to get away for a few hours. It crossed Dougal's mind that Celia would enjoy a small dose of Mr. Pantry's company. But that of course was out of the question.

It had not been difficult to find an excuse to visit the acknowledged doyen of Rosington's scandalmongers. The retired schoolmaster had left his umbrella in Hanbury's Range Rover. Hanbury had telephoned him this morning and suggested that Dougal should return it, since he was coming to Rosington for some shopping. Once Pantry had established that there was no risk of Hanbury dropping in as well, he had issued an enthusiastic invitation to tea.

But the presence of Jonathan Stride at the tea table was something of a complication: it forced Dougal to be much more circumspect. He knew nothing of the man beyond the facts that his absence had been noted at Hanbury's wedding and that Pantry had introduced him as "another of my grateful patients." He was tall and overweight, and had a slight Australian accent. Like Dougal, he had a beard; but, unlike Dougal's, it was a mature growth and neatly trimmed. The hair on his face was perhaps a compensation for the absence of it elsewhere: apart from tufts of hair above the ears, he was entirely bald; the scalp was bronzed and bony. He wore a dark-blue blazer and an unexpectedly garish shirt.

"More tea, anyone? Don't be backward in coming forward."

Pantry left them for a minute to refill the teapot. Almost as if he had been waiting for the opportunity, Stride turned to Dougal.

"I hear you're staying with James. How is he?"

"As you can imagine, he's still a bit shell-shocked. Do you know him well?"

"I used to. We were in the same year, right through Choir School and big school. But it was one of those friendships which lapsed when we went our separate ways. We weren't in the same house at Rosington—though Evelyn seems to think I qualify as an honorary member." Stride glanced sideways at Dougal; a half-smile twitched on his mouth. "You've probably noticed that Evelyn believes one can't have too many grandsons; he's always willing to add another."

"Do you live in Rosington?"

Stride nodded. "I decided to settle here when I got back from Australia a couple of years ago. Purely for sentimental reasons. I've got a house down by the river."

"Now don't be modest, Jon." Pantry set down the teapot and gave Stride a playful pat on the shoulder. "It doesn't suit you, duck. The Old Swan is probably the largest private residence in Rosington after the bishop's palace, and that's hardly private."

Dougal laughed. "Is it an old inn?"

"It was, a long time ago." Stride's face was suddenly alight with enthusiasm. "Until the railways came to Rosington, most goods arrived by river. We had quite a little port down there, and the Old Swan was a combination of hotel and trading post. The core of it is medieval. It was in a terrible state—it had been left to rot for over a century."

"You've made if perfectly delightful," Pantry said firmly. His voice acquired a nuance of interrogation: "And I hate to think what it cost."

Stride refused to be drawn. "It was worth it. Cynthia—my wife, you know—did most of the work. I had a very easy time of it."

"And it will be *such* an appropriate setting for you." Pantry laid a finger along his nose, as if imparting a tremendous secret. He winked roguishly at Dougal. "Entertaining is an important part of the job."

Stride flushed beneath his tan. "There's a possibility I may stand for the Conservatives at the next election," he explained to Dougal. "It hasn't been confirmed yet."

"Pooh!" said Mr. Pantry. "A mere formality. Grandpa knows."

There was a pause in the conversation while their host refilled the cups. On the other side of the wall, a motorbike without a silencer could be heard travelling down Minster Street in the direction of the High Street.

Pantry said: "Those dratted machines!"

"Someone on a motorbike came to Charleston Parva last night," Dougal said casually. "Whoever it was chucked a brick through one of the Dower House windows."

He wondered if he imagined that sudden sideways glance between Pantry and Stride.

"What time was this?" Stride said.

"Getting on for midnight."

Pantry pulled out an elaborate meerschaum pipe and began to fill it. "And did James notify the police?" he asked his tobacco pouch.

Dougal shook his head. "He said there was no point."

"I'm afraid he was perfectly right. There's so much wanton hooliganism in Rosington these days that the police simply don't know where to begin. When you get to Parliament, Jon, I hope you'll do something about it. Bring back the birch. I blame the Welfare State."

Dougal made several other attempts to bring the conversation round to Hanbury, but neither Pantry nor Stride gave him any encouragement. That in itself was curious, for Pantry had apparently been the best of friends with

Hanbury at the wedding. After twenty minutes he gave up.

"I must be going," he said. "I left Sophie in the car and she's probably eaten the steering wheel by now."

Stride glanced at his watch. "I must be off as well. I told Cynthia I'd be back by five. Where have you left your car?"

"In the car park off Bridge Street. I couldn't find anywhere nearer."

"It's always a problem to find anywhere on Saturdays, especially in summer. You get the tourists as well as the shoppers. I'll walk with you."

They said goodbye to Pantry. As they emerged into Minster Street, Stride loosened his tie. At this point the road widened to enclose an egg-shaped patch of scrubby grass, on which stood a weather-beaten public lavatory and a graffiti-daubed telephone box. On the far side of the road was the Porta, the main gateway to the medieval monastery.

Stride nodded towards it. "We might as well go through the Close and cut down through Canons' Meadow."

As they passed through the Porta, they entered a different world. The grumbling of traffic was muted by the high stone walls and the row of trees, chestnuts and copper beeches, which reinforced the barrier between ecclesiastical tranquility and the secular bustle of Minster Street. To their left was the cathedral, visible in its full length, with a huddle of lesser buildings nestling into its flank, as if for protection. In front of them was Canons' Meadow, a large irregular enclosure, studded with trees and pocked with depressions which had once been monastic fishponds, sloping down to Bridge Street and the river.

Stride paused at the iron gate which led to the river. "See that?" He pointed towards the silver streak of water.

"The L-shaped roof with the red tiles? That's the Old Swan. If you're in Rosington around midday tomorrow, come and have some sherry. We usually have a few people round after church." Without any change of tone he added: "I wish I could do something to help James."

Dougal looked sharply at him. "What do you mean?"

"I wasn't entirely frank with you at Pantry's. I did know James very well at school, but we had one hell of a bust-up when we were eighteen. But I really think he should know: there's a great deal of ill-feeling against him in the town. Something nasty could happen."

"Because of Molly's death?"

"She was very well liked. When she got engaged, a lot of people thought James was making a fool of her—that he was just after her money." Stride wiped his forehead. "Maybe he was. And since she died, tongues are wagging even harder, despite the coroner's verdict. If he's got any sense, he'll leave the area. It could be worse than a brick next time."

"And worse than a rotten tomato?"

Stride grinned. "I heard about that. There might be a connection."

"Who threw the tomato?"

"Chap called Peter Carrot. He's our local ne'er-do-well. It's all rather awkward: his aunts are pillars of the community—you may have met them at the wedding. Peter's main aim in life seems to be to *épater les bourgeois* of Rosington. He's very good at it."

"He said 'Look at you!' when he threw the tomato. It sounded like an accusation. I wonder if the 'you' was singular or plural."

Stride moved slowly down the gravel path which bisected the meadow; it was as if he was trying to walk away from the conversation.

Dougal caught up with him. "Has Carrot got a motorbike?"

"As a matter of fact he has. Among his many sins, he's the unofficial leader of the local Hell's Angels." Stride increased his pace. "But don't make too much of it," he said over his shoulder. "Even if there was proof that Carrot was responsible for the brick, I doubt if James would want to prosecute."

"Why on earth not?"

Stride stopped. "If I don't tell you, someone else will. Peter Carrot is popularly believed to be James's illegitimate son."

Four

Dougal could hear Sophie's hysterical yapping from Bridge Street. He turned into the car park and discovered that for once her behaviour was entirely justified.

The black Morris Traveller was in the far corner, largely concealed from view by the van beside it. It was almost certainly the oldest vehicle there. It had belonged to Molly Burnham in the straitened days before she inherited her aunt's wealth. The windows were still covered with faded anti-vivisection stickers. Hanbury had offered Dougal the Range Rover; but Dougal preferred to take the little estate car. The larger and newer a vehicle was, he knew from experience, the more likely he was to hit something with it.

In Dougal's absence, someone had paid a visit with a spray gun of red paint. A row of swastikas staggered along the off-side of the car. On the near-side the word KILLER stretched from one wheel arch to the other.

He unlocked the back of the car, bracing himself just in time. Sophie leapt up, her nose thudding on to his chest, and a wave of foul breath swept over him. He grabbed the collar before she could escape and looped the lead round it. She jumped heavily down, narrowly missing Dougal's feet, and relieved herself in a manner which also only missed Dougal's feet by a narrow margin.

Dougal eventually succeeded in coaxing her back into the car with the help of a raw sausage. He drove out of the car park, trying to ignore the sounds of carnage behind him. Fortunately the Morris, like the Range Rover, was equipped with a grill.

As he left Rosington, he became aware that he had acquired a motorcycle escort. There were three of them —big, glossy machines which instantly aroused Sophie's dislike. At first they rode behind him in single file. Dougal studied them in the rear mirror. The largest of the bikes, a 1000cc juggernaut, had two riders, the others only one. The riders were clothed in black leather and faded denim. Their faces were concealed by helmets with heavy visors.

On the open road, the bikers' tactics changed. They closed in on the car; they swooped to the side and to the front. If any other traffic appeared, they immediately pulled away and became models of automotive decorum.

The rider on the big bike's pillion was a girl. A wisp of dyed blonde hair had escaped from the helmet. She was wearing boots with extremely high heels. When it was the turn of her motorbike to take the lead position she turned in the saddle and extended a small, grubby finger with a bright red nail in an unmistakable gesture of derision and contempt.

Dougal was so scared that his whole body seemed to be vibrating with fear. The rear door and the passenger door were already locked; he locked the driver's door from the inside. Apart from that, he could think of nothing to do except keep driving on at the Morris's top cruising speed of 48 m.p.h. The bikes could go at least twice as fast as he could. If he stopped, he would be at their mercy (whatever that would mean). If he appealed for help from a passing motorist or at one of the villages along the road, the bikers would simply deny everything or disappear; in either case, they could catch him up again when he was alone.

He felt bitterly conscious of his own physical and moral inadequacy. In this last respect, Sophie was undoubtedly his superior. He wondered if she could be trusted to go for them if he told her to. There was always a risk that Sophie might misinterpret the command—through senility, stupidity or sheer bloodymindedness—and go for Dougal instead.

In an agony of indecision he drove on to Charleston Parva, whistling "The British Grenadiers" in a doomed attempt to build his morale.

When he reached the village, however, his escort suddenly left him. He turned left at the crossroads, for the Dower House; the bikes sheered off to the right and vanished beyond the church. Their departure was of course a relief; but it was also something of an anticlimax. Presumably the purpose of the exercise had been to warn him and, through him, Hanbury.

As the crisis dissolved, Mrs. Palmer came out of the village shop. She pointed at the car and said something over her shoulder to someone inside the shop.

Dougal suddenly remembered the graffiti and Jon Stride's message. In one afternoon, he had been given three warnings to relay to Hanbury.

He found Hanbury in the garden, sitting on one cane garden chair with his feet up on another. Beside him on the grass was a motor mower, a tea tray and the slumbering forms of David and Benji.

It took Sophie little more than thirty seconds to destroy this peaceful tableau. While Dougal locked Sophie in the garden shed and unloaded the shopping, Hanbury picked up the fragments of crockery, made some fresh tea and attempted to soothe the Airedales.

The tea, like Mr. Pantry's, proved to be Lapsang, which always tasted to Dougal as an infusion of spiders' webs might. The retired housemaster's influence must still run deep. It occurred to him that Pantry was also responsible for the aura of gentility which Hanbury carried around with him, as ostentatiously as a banner.

But at least Hanbury was drinking tea, not whisky.

"The mower wouldn't start," Hanbury said. "Mrs. Palmer's Wayne used to be the gardener. I expect he sabotaged it on his mother's instructions. Have you had a useful afternoon?"

"I met an old schoolfriend of yours at Pantry's—Jonathan Stride."

"That rat." Hanbury's face grew sullen. "I expect Evelyn let slip you were coming to tea and Stride popped in to see you in the flesh. He always was nosy. What does he look like these days?"

"Prosperous, overweight; bald and bearded. Quite a natty dresser, but his shirt rather spoiled the effect: it clashed with his OR tie."

"That doesn't surprise me," said Hanbury vindictively. "From what I recall of his dress sense, the shirt was probably a violent red-and-green check. Colours are his weak spot."

"Pantry didn't want to talk about you, I'm afraid." Dougal sipped his tea and put the cup down on the grass. With a bit of luck one of the Airedales would knock it over. "But Stride had a message for you: he thinks you should leave the area. He practically said you'd be lynched if you didn't."

Hanbury snorted. "This is England, not the Wild West."

41

"He might not be so far wrong." Dougal mentioned the graffiti and the motorcycle escort. "Perhaps you'd better tell me about Peter Carrot."

"Oh damn. I might have known that old story would surface."

"Is it true that Carrot's your son?"

"Of course not!" Hanbury stared down his nose. "No son of mine could possibly look like that—ah—leather-clad lump."

"Then why is he so interested in you?"

"Dear God." Hanbury reached for his Caporals. "I suppose I shall have to tell you the whole unsavoury story. Not that *I* did anything that could be described as unsavoury. It's a sad comment on human nature, this tendency to believe the worst of anyone. I was guilty of nothing more than—ah—youthful high spirits."

Dougal realized with a shock that Hanbury, possibly the most shameless person he knew, was actually ashamed of, or at least embarrassed by, this episode in his past. The story emerged in fits and starts while Hanbury chainsmoked and swallowed an astonishing quantity of Lapsang Souchong.

It had happened over thirty years before, during Hanbury's last summer term at Rosington School. Hanbury —captain of cricket and head of Pantry's house—had felt he was on the threshold of adulthood; but he was compelled to behave like an overgrown child.

"The location of the school made things worse. I don't know if you know it? It's two or three miles outside Rosington, in the middle of nowhere. Completely isolated from the real world. We had that awful feeling that life was passing us by."

"You said *we*?"

Hanbury nodded. "Myself and two people in the same

42

boat—Jermyn and Stride. They weren't in Pantry's house, but I'd known them since we were eight. Stride was in the choir, and Jermyn was one of the non-singing section of the Choir School. They were pretty wild, even then. They were second cousins, I think—both orphans, no near relatives except their guardian who lived in Australia and frankly couldn't be bothered with them. A psychologist would say their behaviour was a classic attention-seeking strategy. Jermyn was an inspired forger—he used to make a bomb out of doing other people's lines for them, and writing sick notes for day boys."

Dougal felt that the conversation was wandering away from the point; but Hanbury insisted that this was all relevant. As far as Dougal could tell it was relevant only to building up a picture of Hanbury as more sinned against than sinning—a comparative innocent led astray by hardened psychopaths.

"To cut a long story short," Hanbury said with a touch of petulance, "the three of us got into the habit of breaking bounds every evening. We were all prefects, so we didn't have to worry about roll calls. We'd change into—ah—mufti (which was strictly forbidden in itself) and sneak into Rosington on our bikes. We used to go to the Black Pig—it was a pub near the market square which used to attract the rowdier elements; it's an antique shop now. In those days it was full of teddy boys and the odd beatnik. Sometimes the police raided it, which added to the excitement."

Dougal repressed a yawn. His mind was running ahead to the preparation of supper. Could Hanbury be trusted to peel the potatoes? Had Hanbury *ever* peeled a potato?

"And at the centre of all this, my dear William, like —ah—a queen bee holding court, was Alison Carrot."

Hanbury paused and looked expectantly at Dougal,

43

who reluctantly dragged his mind away from the subject of cucumber and yoghurt salad. It was clear that some sort of response was necessary.

"Any connection with Peter?"

"Later, William, later." Hanbury frowned. "Don't be so impatient. Let me deal with Alison first. She was the sort of person you need hyperbole for. For a start, she was *strikingly* attractive—dark, long lashes and—ah—seductive. She was like an exotic orchid among all those dreary little English roses. Secondly—and, believe me, I make this judgement in the light of considerable comparative experience—she was the most evil person I've ever met. And to make it all that much more bizarre—she was a Carrot!"

At that time Hanbury was not personally acquainted with the Carrot family; but no one who had known Rosington thirty years earlier could fail to be unaware of their existence. The patriarch, Ezekiel Carrot, had died two years before, but his shadow still lay over the city. He had been an immensely wealthy businessman and farmer; his principles—he was a teetotal Nonconformist with socialist leanings—brought him into continual conflict with the church authorities. He lived in an ugly Victorian house on the site of what had once been the abbey vineyards. He had three daughters; since their mother's death the two elder sisters had brought up Alison. Always spoiled, she became ungovernable after her father died.

"She was nineteen," Hanbury said, "and she already seemed a woman of the world. We lusted after her, of course, and tried to impress her. She egged us on—I bet the little devil was laughing up her sleeve. Then she dared us to spend the night with her in the cathedral. With two bottles of brandy, some pep pills and a pack of cards."

"How could you get in at night? That place is like a fortress."

44

"The chap who did the stoves had a key to the little door in the north choir aisle. He kept it in a shed the cathedral maintenance men used. Stride and I had known about it for years—we found it when we were choristers. Jermyn stayed with Alison while we went to get it. I remember worrying that she might run off with him while we were gone. I wish to God she had."

The four intruders had made their way through the cathedral to the vestry. Here the windows had black-out curtains, a relic of the war, and it was safe to use the electric light. It was then that Alison had added a new angle to the evening's entertainment: she proposed a game of strip poker. The winner could have her, there and then, on the scarred oak table in the vestry; the losers however, would have to accept whatever penalties she might prescribe for them.

"It so happened that I won."

Dougal, alerted by a hint of smugness in Hanbury's voice, asked if he had cheated.

Hanbury lit another cigarette from the stub of the first. "It seemed—ah—foolish," he said between puffs, "to leave the outcome entirely to chance. Alison let Stride and Jermyn get dressed. Then she told Jermyn to go and break into the moneybox by the west door—we'd found the keys in the vestry—while Stride had to go and get one of the candles from the high altar at the east end. Afterwards they were to wait outside until we'd finished. But unfortunately we didn't really get started. I failed to achieve my aim. The brandy, you know. Or perhaps the excitement—"

"You mean you were impotent when it came to the point?"

Hanbury ignored the question. "The next thing we knew, Jermyn came back with the news that Stride had vanished. It took about twenty minutes to find out

45

that he'd left the cathedral—and locked the door behind him. Alison thought it was a great joke," Hanbury added gloomily. "And she decided to share it with Jermyn."

"Are you saying that Jermyn must be Peter Carrot's father?"

"It's probable, but by no means certain. The time fits—Peter was born in March; but we don't know whether Alison was—ah—celibate before and after that night."

Hanbury, Alison and Jermyn had managed to slip out of the cathedral unnoticed at six thirty, when the head verger made his rounds. But once they were out of the cathedral precincts, their luck changed. They ran into a search party composed of Alison's sisters, Evelyn Pantry and Leo Cumblesham, who was at that time a housemaster at Rosington. The empty brandy bottles told their own story; fortunately there was no need to mention the pep pills, the cathedral or the strip poker and its consequences.

"It was all hushed up, of course. Pantry and Cumblesham knew that Jermyn and I would be leaving in a fortnight; the Carrot sisters would perjure themselves to God almighty where Alison was concerned; no one wanted scandal. By the time Alison's pregnancy became obvious, Jermyn and I were out of harm's way."

Dougal stood up. "I must start doing something about dinner."

"I'd offer to help. But I'm such a duffer in the kitchen."

"It's never too late to learn."

"I should really take David and Benji for a walk. Another time, perhaps."

Dougal shrugged. In normal circumstances he would have persisted. But the size of the cheque which Hanbury had given him that morning held him back. Hanbury had called it a week's wages in advance; the sum involved was so generous that it might reasonably be supposed to include cooking and general housekeeping duties as well as research. He picked up the tea-tray.

"By the way," he said. "If both you and Jermyn were caught with Alison, why is everyone so ready to assume that you were the one who fathered Peter?"

"Alison said it was me before she decamped from Rosington." Hanbury jingled the Airedales' leads and they leapt up. "God knows why. Possibly on the principle that you don't speak ill of the dead. But it's much more likely that she was contemplating getting money from the father, perhaps through the court. Dead fathers can't pay."

Mr. Pantry was conversing with God.

Dougal watched with interest. He was sitting on the cantorial side of the choir, beneath the jagged pipes of the organ. Mr. Pantry was directly opposite, on the decanal or south side; like Dougal he occupied one of the topmost tier of stalls.

Unlike Dougal, Pantry was praying. His beaked nose protruded through his long white fingers. On the smallest finger of his left hand was a gold signet ring with what looked like an emerald in it. He was dressed in a light grey suit with the finest of pinstripes. His shirt cuffs and handkerchief were snowy white. The grey hair had been so cleverly combed that the bald patch was hardly visible across the choir.

Above their heads the great Victorian organ of Rosington thundered an impressive accompaniment to Mr. Pantry's devotions. Most of the other worshippers had either left or were in the process of going. Dougal joined the stragglers and found himself, as he had intended, beside Mr. and Mrs. Stride.

Cynthia Stride bowed in a stately but civil fashion to

Dougal when her husband introduced him. The stateliness was a triumph against nature, since she was a short, stout woman.

"How do you do, Mr. Dougal? A researcher? How interesting. You must tell me all about it some time. Have you time to join us for a glass of sherry? *A bientôt*, then: I must have a word with my father."

Mrs. Stride hurried away beneath the great dome of the octagon towards the vestry, from which one of the officiating clergy—a small, portly priest in a cassock which was green with age—was emerging.

"Canon Westmoreland," Stride explained. "I expect he'll be joining us at the Old Swan."

There was a note of subdued satisfaction in his voice, which Dougal decided must relate to his political ambitions. In a town like Rosington, an alliance with the church was not to be despised. The marriage, Dougal guessed, had probably taken place since Stride's return from Australia.

Stride's guests trailed in twos and threes through the cathedral precincts, down Canons' Meadow and across Bridge Street to the Old Swan. The inn was built of crumbling yellow stone round two sides of a courtyard. The courtyard, through which the guests passed to reach the front door, had been turned into a walled garden.

Stride led the way into a sitting room which occupied the whole of the ground floor of the wing parallel to the river. It was a long, beamed room whose floor was several feet below the outside ground level. On the side away from the courtyard, small mullioned windows looked across a towpath to the river.

Two large trays were waiting on the refectory table to the right of the door. One held glasses and decanters, the other an array of nuts, biscuits and dainty, bite-sized snacks.

The Strides evidently subscribed to the bread-and-circuses school of political philosophy.

Soon there were nearly twenty people in the sitting room, sipping, nibbling and talking. Dougal found himself next to Canon Westmoreland. The Canon, a veteran of such social gatherings, had acquired two glasses of sherry and a plate loaded with a selection of food. He stockpiled these on the table beside him. As they chatted, his pudgy fingers moved deftly among the edibles, conveying morsels to his open mouth.

"Cynthia tells me you're a researcher, Mr. Um . . . What do you research?"

"Anything that comes along—usually historical. I work on a freelance basis for a publisher who does a lot of popular history books. It's a sort of package deal: someone famous puts his name on the cover and is meant to do the actual writing; someone else does the picture research; and I quarry out the detail."

"And what have you been working on lately?" the Canon enquired between mouthfuls.

"I've just finished a biography of Cromwell." It was in fact the first and only piece of work Dougal had done; but there seemed no point in mentioning this.

"Dear me. Not a popular person around here. He stabled his horses in the nave, you know. We used to have rather a nice Decorated rood screen until he set his Ironsides loose on it. Wretched man."

More than three centuries had passed since these desecrations, but Westmoreland's indignation was as fresh as if it had happened yesterday. In his agitation he forgot that his mouth was full: several fragments of cashewnut landed on Dougal's lapel. Dougal recoiled unobtrusively, wishing that the biography had dealt with a less controversial subject.

The Canon, perhaps embarrassed by his own vehemence, hastened to change the subject. "Jon and Cynthia have done some splendid work here," he boomed. "A few years ago this place was derelict. The council wanted to pull it down and use the ground for a car park or some such nonsense. Do you live locally, Mr. Um?"

Dougal shook his head. "I'm staying with a friend," he said vaguely; "I live in London."

His caution was ruined by the arrival of Evelyn Pantry, who was making a tour round the room for the purposes of disseminating and gathering information.

"Good morning, Clarence. Good morning, Mr. Dougal." He put his head on one side and added in a stage whisper: "I see James isn't here. *Very* wise, if I may say so. *Such* a lovely morning. Janet Carrot wasn't in church today. Migraine, perhaps. Unless she was at the eight o'clock."

"James?" The cocktail sausage in Westmoreland's hand paused outside his mouth. "You're staying with James Hanbury?"

Dougal nodded.

The Canon put the sausage in his mouth and picked up his glass. "Must have a word with Cynthia about the um. Excuse me."

Mr. Pantry raised an eyebrow at Westmoreland's retreat. "Oh dear. I'm afraid the Chapter at Rosington are rather *conservative* in their views. I must apologize: I've made you guilty by association."

"A sort of social leprosy?" Dougal suggested.

But Pantry's attention had been diverted towards fresh prey. He touched the elbow of a tall, thin woman with lank grey hair which trailed raggedly over her collar.

"Julia! Someone said Janet had one of her migraines. I do hope not."

"Not a migraine." Julia stared incuriously at Dougal;

50

her large brown eyes were out of place in that pinched, grey face; they should have been in a face which was twenty years younger and glowing with vitality. "We had rather a shock last night: Alison rang up. It must be the first time in fifteen years."

"Good Heavens! You don't think—But I'm forgetting my manners. Julia, this is William Dougal; he's staying with James at the Dower House. William—I may call you William, mayn't I? I'm old enough to be your grandfather—this is Mrs. Westmoreland, the Canon's daughter-in-law."

Julia edged closer to Dougal. " 'Stand in awe, and sin not,' " she said earnestly. "Psalm four. I hope James isn't letting himself go."

Dougal said he didn't think there was much risk of that.

Pantry could contain himself no longer: "But *why* did Alison telephone you?"

Julia shrugged. "Alison never says why she does things." The fervour had left her voice and the eyes were dull. "She rang us up to announce that she was coming to stay at the Vineyards on Monday. That's why Janet wasn't in church. She's far too busy communing with the fatted calf to bother about God."

Five

Sophie stood in the bows, barking indiscriminately at boats, ducks, pedestrians and passing cars. Once they were out of the city, however, she calmed down. She slumped inelegantly on her side and began to snore.

Dougal punted onwards upstream. Every now and then he glanced back at the spire of the cathedral. There was no chance of losing sight of it; the flatness of the Fens made it visible for miles around.

Punting was one of the few physical accomplishments which Dougal could trust his body to perform with unspectacular but persistent competence; it was one of the lasting benefits he had gained from a misspent university education. He had noticed the punts and canoes on the river at the Old Swan. Julia Westmoreland had told him where they could be hired. A riverside pub had supplied his lunch—a pork pie, which Sophie had already eaten, and a can of chilled lager.

There was no hurry to get back to Charleston Parva, for Hanbury was not expecting him back early. Dougal felt he deserved a little holiday: in the last two days, he had began to pine for his own company.

The river was wide and sluggish. Dougal kept to the

left-hand bank, since the boatman had warned him that the punt pole had no chance of touching bottom in mid-stream. When he had gone nearly a mile without meeting any other craft in either direction, he decided it was safe to moor. He steered into the bank and ran the punt's bows beneath the drooping branches of a willow tree. He secured the stern with the pole, stepped into the centre of the punt and sat down on the cushions.

Sophie stirred as he cracked open the lager, but mer-cifully did not come to investigate. Dougal lay back, with one hand trailing in the water. He squinted up, through half-closed eyes, at the willow and the sun behind it. Rainbows danced along his eyelashes.

He sat up to light a cigarette. As the match flared, a disturbing image invaded his mind: he suddenly remem-bered the warm brown eyes of Julia Westmoreland, set in that tortured face. The vividness of the contrast abruptly dispelled his feeling that the afternoon could be set aside for rest-and-recreation. It was difficult to relax with someone else's blatant unhappiness cluttering up your mind.

He seized on the nearest distraction, which was the job on hand. It seemed pretentious to call it a "case" or an "investigation": nothing he had discovered justified so grandiose a title. But this was still a job; and Dougal's streak of obstinacy made him want to finish something once he had started it.

The traditional trio of headings—means, motive and opportunity—seemed the simplest way to regiment his thought processes, though he felt a trifle self-conscious about using the hallowed trinity of crime detection in this matter.

The means of death had never been in dispute. The question was whether their use had been accidental or intentional. Dougal had gone over the same ground as the police, and had found nothing which contradicted their conclusion. On the other hand, it was undoubtedly true that anyone with a modicum of intelligence could have booby-trapped the wiring in a manner which concealed that it had been tampered with. Dougal had taken apart the twin of the killer-lamp. The candlestick base unscrewed into three sections; the flex inside zigzagged up to the socket, and much of its insulation had cracked with age—and in some places had peeled away altogether. It would have been a simple matter to ensure that one of the bare places was lodged against the brass tracery of the candlestick's shaft.

Tinkering with the fuse box would have required some attention to detail. The wire which replaced the original fuse would ideally have come from an old electrical appliance. The perpetrator would have had to take particular care not to leave fresh scratches or scars on the brass screws which clamped the fuses within their porcelain containers. But it *could* have been done: Dougal had tried the experiment himself, using an electrical screwdriver whose tip he had padded with the corner of a handkerchief.

Though Dougal felt confident that common sense and a little basic electrical knowledge could have converted the lamp into a lethal weapon, only one shred of evidence suggested that someone might actually have done so. The shred was so insubstantial that Dougal hadn't even mentioned it to Hanbury. In the overhead light of the study he had found a dud, clear-glass, 100 watt bulb; but 60 watt pearl bulbs, of a different brand, were used elsewhere in the house. It was just conceivable that a hypothetical murderer, wishing to make quite sure that someone would use the lamp as soon as possible, had taken the trouble to remove a working bulb from the overhead light and to replace it with a broken one, which he or she had presumably brought to the house for that purpose.

The question of opportunity produced too many answers for Dougal's peace of mind. Everyone above an invisible social waterline in Rosington and its environs seemed to be familiar with the Dower House. Most of these would have known that the room on the right of the front door was to be Hanbury's study, for the matter had been thoroughly aired at the party at which Molly and Hanbury had announced their engagement. Everyone who could afford a copy of the *Rosington Observer* knew that the Hanburys were spending a month in Sri Lanka after their wedding. The presence of the key beneath a cracked flowerpot on the kitchen windowsill was almost equally widely known.

As for the timing of the death, this must have been left to chance. The hypothetical murderer would have assumed that Hanbury would be the first to try the light, since the room was meant to be his sanctum. But a malicious fate had sent Molly in there instead. There were a dozen possible reasons why she might have gone there—to fetch some paper, to look for a book, to plan alterations to the decor.

Dougal lit another cigarette and turned to the matter of motive. He could find none for Molly's death. She seemed to have been universally well liked; Hanbury had provided documentary evidence to prove that he had little or nothing to gain financially from her death—he had already managed to gain effective control of the purse strings.

A more plausible assumption was that Hanbury was the intended victim. Given that the murder would have required extensive local knowledge, it followed that the murderer probably came from the Burnham-Hanbury circle of acquaintance in and around Rosington. According to Hanbury, money could not be the motive—Molly was, or had been, his sole beneficiary. (And it was absurd, Dougal added parenthetically, to imagine that Molly would have set up a trap to kill her own husband, only to fall into it herself.)

Hanbury was certainly unpopular in Rosington—but much of this ill-feeling stemmed directly from Molly's death. A few people had specific reasons to wish him out of the way, though none of the reasons seemed weighty enough to provide the motive for a premeditated murder. Jon Stride, on the verge of a political career, might find it mildly embarrassing if Hanbury revealed he had participated in an ill-starred schoolboy orgy in the cathedral. Janet Carrot and/or her sister Julia Westmoreland might nurture murderous designs on Hanbury for debauching their beloved Alison. By the same token, Peter Carrot—whose distaste for his putative father was obvious—might have tried to express his dislike as definitively as possible; after all, one could only go so far with a brick or a tomato.

Sophie twitched, opened one eye and yawned. Dougal yawned in response. He dropped his cigarette end in the can, where it fizzled itself to extinction in the dregs of lager. He might have missed Sunday lunch, but the traditional Sunday afternoon stupor was catching up on him.

His eyelids drooped over his eyes. As he fell asleep, it occurred to him that Hanbury had not told him where he had been on the evening that Molly was killed.

Was it unusual to leave your wife alone on the first night after your honeymoon?

Dougal got back to the Dower House at four o'clock. The first thing he noticed was that someone had left a white Mercedes in the courtyard.

He went in through the kitchen door. The Airedales were asleep under the table; Sophie flung herself towards them with a playful snarl. Dougal slipped into the hall.

There were voices coming through the open door of the sitting room.

"Ah—William." Hanbury paused in the act of pouring a cup of tea: the stream of Lapsang became a dribble. "This is William Dougal," he said to the woman who sat in the armchair opposite his. He turned back to William. "And this is Madame Volin. Would you like some tea?"

"No, thanks." Dougal shook hands with their guest. She was a well-preserved woman in her forties, by the look of her, with short dark hair and a face which was better than beautiful. She wore jeans, a loose T-shirt and sandals; the perfect simplicity of her clothes was a better guarantee of her secure financial status than the Mercedes. Her only jewellery was a gold wedding band.

"Madame Volin rang me from Cambridge just after you left. A delightful surprise. She's at the University Arms."

Dougal scratched his beard. He had seen Madame Volin's eyes only a few hours ago, in someone else's face. Hanbury had, once again, forgotten to be entirely frank with him.

"Madame Volin," Dougal said softly, "I suppose you must be Alison Carrot?"

She grinned at him. "Of course. James was right."

Hanbury chuckled. "I told Alison you were sharp. But how did you know?"

"I met Julia Westmoreland at the Strides' this morning. The eyes are the same. Besides, she mentioned her sister was expected at the Vineyards tomorrow."

"And now you're thinking the worst of me. Alison, would you explain to my young friend what happened?"

Madame Volin smiled at Dougal; it was the sort of smile which could launch a thousand ships or stop a man dead at fifty paces. "I flew in from Paris last night. I thought

57

I'd better give my family a little warning so I decided to spend a couple of nights in a hotel. I rang James this morning"—a laugh bubbled out of her—"from curiosity, I suppose. How are my sisters?"

"I only saw Mrs. Westmoreland. Miss Carrot stayed at home this morning."

"How entirely typical. Each of them has their own way of responding to a crisis: Janet cleans the silver and Julia rushes out to tell someone."

Alison Volin laughed again; it was at this moment that Dougal began to dislike her.

Hanbury, as if sensing something was amiss, said: "I'm sure they will be delighted to see you. Will your husband be coming over to join you?"

"Paul never goes anywhere unless it's on business." Madame Volin dismissed her husband from the conversation with a plausible imitation of a Gallic shrug. "I hope to God Janet's cooking has improved over the last twenty years."

Dougal abandoned all pretence at subtlety. "Mrs. Westmoreland was wondering why you were coming back after so long."

Alison tried the smile on him again. "Nostalgia, I suppose. I saw that Molly and James were getting married —I take *The Times*, you see, just to keep in touch. Then I saw that she had died. Molly and I were great friends when we were children. It made me wonder what I'd left behind."

She left soon afterwards, having arranged for them to dine with her the following Wednesday, at a time and place to be settled later. Hanbury waved until she was out of sight. Then he wiped his face.

"Come and sit in the garden, William. The sitting room stinks of *Je Reviens*. Come on, admit it: you thought I was playing a double game."

Dougal nodded.

Hanbury sat down on the more robust of the two deckchairs. "I promise you—her arrival came as a complete shock to me. That phone call this morning brought me out in a cold sweat. I tell you one thing: she's no more Madame Volin than I am."

"But it *is* Alison?" Dougal took one of Hanbury's Caporals. "And how do you know she isn't Madame Volin?"

"I'm not a complete innocent. I went through her handbag when she was in the loo. The stupid woman should have taken it with her. Passport, credit cards, French identity card—all in the name of Alison Garance."

"Why's she using a pseudonym?"

"It might have something to do with the fact that Jean-Paul Garance came up for trial in Paris last month. I think he got ten years. He's a rather talented computer hacker; I believe they call him a "vault invader." He and his friends used the salami method to siphon off about five million francs from three of the major clearing banks. Alison may be feeling the financial pinch. By the look of her, she's accustomed to a certain style of living."

"I thought all the Carrot sisters had money of their own."

"By the standards of thirty years ago, they were wealthy. Janet and Julia are still comfortably off, at a guess. But I doubt if Alison's got much left of her share."

Dougal blew two smoke rings. In the distance, the dogs were clamouring for food. Alison's arrival made a little more sense if she was here for financial, rather than sentimental reasons. Did Hanbury realize that he himself—now rich in his own right—might be one of the targets selected by the grass widow of Paris?

"She said she got here last night. D'you think that was the truth?"

Hanbury looked up sharply, with a frown on his face. "You don't think—?"

"Do you?"

"Nothing in her handbag confirmed or denied what she said. But it's surely a bit—ah—far-fetched to suggest that she murdered Molly so that she could then latch on to me and Molly's money."

"Just a thought." Dougal brooded for a moment. "It's odd how all the people who were concerned in your little escapade in the cathedral are drifting back to Rosington. You've all come back now—except Jermyn, of course. What happened to him?"

"Old Charles died ages ago. A year or two after we left school, I think. I was abroad—we had National Service in those days—but I saw the news in the *Rosingtonian*; they send the school magazine to old boys who are stupid enough to sign on for life membership of the OR Society."

"But how did he die?"

"I don't think it said. I think there was just an announcement about a forthcoming memorial service. Ask Pantry: he'll know." Dougal called on Mr. Pantry on Monday afternoon. He was unreasonably annoyed to discover that the old man was out. The weather matched his mood: the sunshine of the weekend had disappeared overnight; a fine but penetrating rain drifted down from the grey sky.

As he turned away, he caught sight of Julia Westmoreland struggling up the hill which led down to the station. She was laden with a shopping bag, whose weight dragged her whole body sideways; and in the other hand was a large white cardboard box which she steadied on her hip. She was hatless, and the rain had played havoc with her hair; she looked like a bedraggled Medusa who was dying for a cup of tea.

60

Dougal grabbed his umbrella from the car. As he crossed the green towards her, he saw that her mouth was working: judging by her expression, she was quarrelling violently with an invisible companion.

"May I give you a lift, Mrs. Westmoreland?"

The vindictive expression immediately vanished from the long, angular face. She sidled under the umbrella, bringing herself uncomfortably close to him.

"I'd be *so* grateful. Mr. Dougal, isn't it?"

"Let me take your bag."

They effected the transfer with difficulty, because of the weight of the bag. Dougal suppressed an involuntary shiver as their hands touched. Inside the bag, glass clinked, and he glimpsed the tops of four bottles. The fatted calf was to be washed down with strong waters.

The Morris Traveller was outside Pantry's front door. Mrs. Westmoreland caught sight of the swastikas. Her arms tightened around the cardboard box, which she now held against her flat chest.

"That was Molly's car, wasn't it? Whoever did that to it?"

"Random vandals, I suppose." Dougal decided not to mention that her nephew Peter was the likeliest candidate. "I left it in the Bridge Street car park the other day. It was like that when I got back."

He shepherded her round to the near side of the car and opened the passenger door for her. Here she saw the word KILLER which complemented the swastikas.

"It's disgusting." She clambered awkwardly into the car. "No one has any standards these days. Nothing but animals with diseased minds. James is being persecuted."

Dougal went round to the other side of the car, put the shopping bag and the umbrella on the back seat, and climbed in beside her. Sophie was barking in the back, which forced him to raise his voice.

"You don't subscribe to the idea that James is some sort of Bluebeard?"

It was not a conventional question to ask of a woman whom you hardly knew, but Dougal felt oddly certain that his companion was not in the mood for social niceties.

"Of course not!" Then, with a venom which made the comparison with Medusa seem unexpectedly apt, she added: "It's all the fault of my little sister."

"I don't quite follow you."

"Alison smears everyone she touches. Janet could never see that. But I learnt it the hard way." She tapped the box on her bosom. "You know what this is? Chocolate cake. Alison's favourite, so Janet insisted I went out for it. Not just *any* chocolate cake, either: it has to come from Rider's, which is miles away, down by the station. And who has to go and fetch it? Why, poor old muggins, of course."

"James isn't liked because"—Dougal cast around for an acceptable circumlocution—"because people believe he led Alison astray?"

Julia Westmoreland nodded vigorously. " 'An unwise man does not well consider this: and a fool doth not understand it,' " she said in a high, nasal voice. "Psalm ninety-two. It was the other way round."

"I see." Dougal twisted the key in the ignition. "I don't suppose you know where I could find Mr. Pantry?"

"He'll be at the Vineyards. Janet's organizing a welcome-home tea party." Her face suddenly twisted. "You come as well. No reason why I shouldn't have my own guests."

"Thanks. I'd like that." Dougal started the engine and drove carefully down Minster Street. He had no particular desire to have tea at the Vineyards; and Janet Carrot was unlikely to welcome him. But he was becoming increasingly curious about these emotional cross-currents which seethed beneath the placid surface of Rosington. This was too good a chance to turn down. Hanbury would be fascinated to have an eye-witness report of Alison's homecoming.

"Stop!" screamed Mrs. Westmoreland as they turned into the High Street.

Dougal, expecting to find at least one old age pensioner crushed beneath his wheels, stabbed his foot on the brake. The car behind him hooted.

"Just pull over, will you? I forgot the lemons. Madame must have her slice of lemon in her gin-and-tonic."

He parked on a double yellow line and waited, keeping an anxious watch for traffic wardens, while Julia Westmoreland went into the greengrocer's.

There was a rap on the nearside front window. It seemed to have been caused by a large expanse of bright blue, semitransparent plastic. He leant over the seat, narrowly avoiding the chocolate cake, and rolled down the window.

Cynthia Stride's round face, framed in a hood which matched the rest of her plastic raincoat, appeared in the gap.

"It's Mr. Um, isn't it?" She had inherited her memory for names from her father. "Thought I recognized Molly's car. Pity about the graffiti, though. Have you seen my husband?"

Dougal shook his head.

"It's most annoying. He said he would meet me in the library at half-past three—Ah, Julia. Have *you* seen Jon?"

Mrs. Westmoreland, a lemon in each hand, asked where Cynthia had lost him.

"Very droll, dear. I left him at home an hour ago. We

were going to meet at the library after I'd done my shopping, and come on to the Vineyards together. I can't think where he's got to."

"Perhaps he's already there." Julia got into the car and put an end to the conversation by rolling up the window. "I know she's my sister-in-law, but I can't stand that woman. Never could. 'Whoso hath also a proud look and high stomach: I will not suffer him.' Psalm a hundred and one."

Dougal drove on up the High Street, round the market square and into the gravelled forecourt of the Vineyards. There were already half a dozen cars parked there. Beside the white Mercedes was Hanbury's Range Rover.

Six

Hanbury snuffed the air, like a warhorse preparing for battle.

"*Calèche*, I fancy." He bowed over Alison's hand as he shook it, contriving to suggest that only the English provincialism of their environment prevented him from kissing it. "They say it's Elizabeth Taylor's favourite perfume. I think I prefer it to the more robust *Je Reviens* you wore yesterday. It implies much, but discreetly says little."

Hanbury had spoken in a clearly audible voice, and his words caused an instant's complete silence in the big, first-floor drawing room of the Vineyards. Then several conversations began at once; but it was noticeable that most of the other guests kept their eyes trained on the bay window.

It had been adroit, Dougal admitted to himself as he shook Alison's hand for the second time in twenty-four hours. With a single conversational gambit, Hanbury had flattered Alison, impressed upon the assembled citizenry that he and she shared a sophistication which they did not possess, demonstrated that Alison bore him no grudge because she had seen him yesterday before seeing anyone else, and triumphantly declined to be treated like a pariah.

Hanbury, in other words, was back on form.

Julia presented her cheek for Alison to peck. Evelyn Pantry, perhaps the most sensitive social barometer in Rosington, swooped towards the group in the window.

"James, dear boy. I haven't seen you for days. You haven't been ill, I hope?"

Hanbury seized the proferred olive branch. "A touch of flu. Nothing serious, but enough to keep me at home for a few days. William's been keeping an eye on me."

"Flu?" said Canon Westmoreland who, teacup in hand, had sidled up behind them. "There's a lot of it about. The Bishop had a very bad go of it last month."

Dougal slipped away and joined the little queue in front of the teapot. He received a cup of tea and was turning to go when a podgy little man beside him jogged his elbow. Tea slopped into his saucer. Both of them apologized. The man wore a tight, dark suit which had been fashionable five years ago, an Old Rosingtonian tie and a pair of gold-rimmed National Health glasses. Dougal realized with a shock that he was talking to the bourgeois incarnation of Peter Carrot.

"Let's go and have a real drink," Carrot said abruptly. "Can't stand these vicarage tea parties."

Dougal followed him downstairs to the dining room. It was a cheerless place, full of huge mahogany furniture; fresh polish partly concealed the underlying odours of old food; the window looked on to an unkempt garden.

Carrot raided the sideboard and came back with two cans of bitter. He slid one across the table to Dougal, scarring a line across the surface. They sat down opposite one another, which brought an odd touch of formality to the proceedings. *The board meeting*, Dougal thought, *is about to begin.*

"It's a bloody laugh, isn't it?" Carrot took a long pull

of his beer and burped. "You realize my *parents* are up there? And both of them look straight through me, as if I didn't exist. I tell a lie: my mother looked at me for about two seconds. Dear old ma who hasn't seen me for thirty-odd years. Know what she said?" His voice became a horrible parody of his mother's, complete with the hint of French accent: " '*We must see about getting your hair cut, dear.*' "

Dougal took a cigarette and pushed the packet towards his host. "Why did you come?"

"Aunt Janet was sure there'd be a touching reconciliation. All this"—he tugged at the pink and silver tie—"was her idea. I feel a right prat."

Carrot lit a cigarette and scratched his armpit vigorously. His pupils were dilated, Dougal noticed, and his movements jerky. Dougal asked him if he lived here still.

"No—I got out years ago. Sally and I got a council flat over the river."

"The blonde on the motorbike?"

Carrot's eyes swivelled towards him. "We weren't after you," he said with a trace of embarrassment. "Just a way of telling that bugger Hanbury he's unwanted round here."

"I think he got your message. That one and the others. Why are you so sure he's your father?"

Dougal hoped he hadn't gone too far. His intuition told him that Peter Carrot was in a state of shock; and experience suggested he was speeding as well. He needed to talk; and he had seized on Dougal as the only available stranger of about his own age.

"Why should I tell you? You're his friend."

"But that doesn't mean I'm your enemy," Dougal said evenly.

Carrot shrugged. "Everyone says it was him. Have you any idea what it's like? People look sideways at you.

My aunts tried to pretend I was just like everyone else, but it didn't work. All the kids at school knew. They used to call me 'little bastard.' "

"But you stayed in Rosington. You could have left."

"There's nowhere else to go. Besides, there's some fun in rubbing their noses in it. 'Oh my dear!' " he fluted in an excruciating falsetto, " 'A Carrot living with a dust-man's daughter! Convicted for drug-pushing! Brawling in the Crossed Keys!' " His voice returned to its normal pitch. "It has its moments. I tell you, if I had a bomb, I'd drop it on Rosington. Obliterate it. Just think of it: this whole town reduced to *nothing*."

"Even Sally?"

Carrot considered the question quite seriously. "I'd spare her. She's worth ten of everyone upstairs put to-gether." He jabbed his thumb towards the ceiling. "*They're* the people who should die. And I'd start with my mother and my aunts." He leant forward confidentially. "The Carrots are mad, you know—it's well known in the town. People say that my grandpa, old Ezekiel, was the son of a brother and a sister. It used to happen a lot on farms round here." He flicked ash on the dull red carpet. "Julia's a religious nut who hates the other two. She used to worship my ma until dear old mummy ran off with her husband. Frank Westmoreland, the Canon's son. They say he's a bartender on the Costa del Sol now. Aunt Janet, on the other hand—she's into power. Me and my mother are her favourite dolls. But her real pleasure comes from playing the heavy with Julia. Julia's too pathetic to do anything about it except quote psalms about her behind her back. They're all insane, I tell you."

The amphetamine-inspired eloquence suddenly dried up. Carrot stared at his blurred reflection in the highly polished table; he swung his head from side to side like a bull about to charge. Dougal got up to fetch an ashtray from the sideboard.

"Maybe it would be best if you went home now," he said gently.

Carrot ignored the suggestion. "Something's going to happen—I can feel it. My mother's—what do you call something that changes quickly?"

"Volatile?"

"Volatile. O-level chemistry and all that. Now she's back, there's going to be an explosion. Good thing, perhaps—rip this smug little town to shreds." His train of thought had come full circle. "That's what we need —a bomb."

His arm swept out in a wide arc to emphasize what he said. His elbow collided with his beer: the can fell over and rolled a few inches; beer spurted across the table.

Dougal righted the can. He was trying hard to be a calm, authoritative father-figure; but he lacked some vital ingredient. He reissued the one constructive suggestion he could think of.

"I really think you should go home."

"A very sensible idea," said a voice from the doorway. "Run along now, Peter."

Dougal and Carrot swung round as Evelyn Pantry came into the room. The door had been ajar: Dougal wondered how much of the conversation the old man had over-heard.

"Off you go. You'll feel better in the morning. Have a good hot bath when you get home."

Carrot stumbled to his feet. "Yes . . ." The word ended in a hiss, as if he was about to add "sir" but had stopped himself just in time. He walked out of the room without a glance at Dougal. A few seconds later, the front door slammed behind him.

Dougal looked at Pantry with a certain amount of respect. The old schoolmaster had the knack of authority, for all his absurdities. "Old habits die hard?"

Pantry waved his hand in a manner which displayed his signet ring to the best advantage. "Oh yes, duck! Grandpa can still do it, if he has to. If one treats Peter as if he was fourteen, one can't go far wrong."

"Were you coming to rescue me?"

"I thought you might need it. Janet was really rather silly to ask Peter. It was asking for trouble. If he'd gone back upstairs, he'd've had one of his tantrums. Oh dear: it's not a happy home."

Dougal stubbed out his cigarette. He found a paper handkerchief in his pocket and mopped up as much of the spilt beer as he could. He dropped the sodden handkerchief in the ashtray. Pantry, meanwhile, had strolled across to the window. Dougal joined him. The garden sloped down to a wall of weathered red brick. Beyond it, the roofs of the town, glistening with rain, descended in tiers down to the level of the surrounding Fens.

"James is making quite a fuss of Alison," Pantry murmured. "Perhaps a *little* unwise. Cynthia Stride was being rather rude about it. But she's peeved because Jon was called away on council business, out of the blue. She likes to parade her husband in public, as you've probably noticed. It was a late marriage, and she's terribly possessive."

Dougal wondered why Pantry was being so forthcoming with him, like so many people he had met in Rosington. It was as if everyone in this closed society was trying to enrol him, a newcomer, on his or her side before someone else managed to grab his allegiance. The social politics of Rosington bore a considerable resemblance to those of the playground on the one hand, and the United

Nations on the other. Dougal thought of himself as an unaligned Third World country. But Pantry's next words revealed that there was another reason for his confidences.

"Tell me, William, have Alison and James been—how shall I put it—seeing one another before today? They seemed to imply . . ." Pantry raised his eyebrows and laid a hand on Dougal's arm. "I know for a fact that Janet is very put out."

Dougal had no objection, in principle, to trading information for information. "She phoned him yesterday and invited herself to tea at the Dower House. As far as I know, they hadn't met for thirty years."

"How very interesting." The little eyes behind the thick glasses were hard and shrewd.

"Talking of thirty years ago," Dougal said before Pantry could probe further, "James was wondering how his friend Jermyn died."

"Ah *yes*." Pantry's eyelashes fluttered, and his grip tightened on Dougal's arm. "Charles Jermyn, bless my soul. He's the only one who's missing from this little reunion."

A sly smile flickered across the wrinkled face. Dougal felt a twitch of revulsion. In profile the old man looked like a bald-headed vulture eating a morsel of scandal. In the wrinkles, Dougal could see traces of face powder.

"How did he die?" Dougal prompted.

"It was very sad," Pantry said. "The poor duck was so young. He was murdered, I'm afraid. I believe some tramp killed him for the sake of a few pounds."

"Where did it happen?"

"Oh, nowhere round *here*." Pantry pursed his mouth as if indicating that distance from Rosington necessarily diminished the event's importance. "I believe it was somewhere near Cheltenham."

"But there was a memorial service here."

71

"Well, the school felt it had to do something. Poor Charles was quite alone in the world."

"I thought there was a guardian or something."

"He died in Australia a few months earlier. No, Charles's only relation was Jon Stride—and he was in Australia himself by that time. They insisted I did the address at the service. An ill-favoured thing, no doubt, but mine own. The headmaster wanted to print the text in the next *Rosingtonian*."

Pantry was perfectly prepared to talk at length about the memorial service or indeed about any other triumph in his long career; but Dougal could glean no more about the manner of Jermyn's death. He found it impossible to judge whether Pantry's stonewalling concealed ignorance or reticence. After five minutes of the old man's autobiography, Dougal gently freed his arm and suggested that they rejoin the rest of the party.

The atmosphere in the drawing room had undergone a change in Dougal's absence. More people had arrived, and tea had been abandoned in favour of alcohol. Voices were louder; peels of laughter came from the group around Hanbury and Alison. Dougal sidled closer and discovered that Canon Westmoreland was complimenting Alison on her appearance.

Julia Westmoreland touched Dougal's arm. " 'Their throat is an open sepulchre,' " she confided. " 'They flatter with their tongue.' Psalm five."

Hanbury, meanwhile, was telling a humorous anecdote which involved a cabinet minister of his acquaintance and a celebrated actress. Cynthia Stride capped it with a story whose chief purpose seemed to be to demonstrate that she and her husband were also on first-name terms with the same minister.

Dougal circulated round the room, touching on the

fringes of the other groups but declining to be drawn into their orbits. He was beginning to understand how Peter Carrot felt about Rosington's leading citizens. Their abiding passions seemed to be curiosity and malice. Outsiders were welcome only if they observed the rules.

Hanbury broke away from Alison. "William! Have another drink. Don't look so doleful, dear boy—this is a party."

Like anyone else, Dougal objected to being called doleful, even if he was. Before he could reply, however, Janet Carrot surged between them. Her ample form was swathed in imperial purple; her chubby face was flushed with exertion and, perhaps, with irritation.

"Mr. Dougal?" she said accusingly. "It *is* Mr. Dougal, isn't it? There's a phone call for you. A young"—her nose twitched—"lady."

Hope, as irrational as it was powerful, surged through him: *It must be Celia.* Common sense immediately murdered hope.

The phone was downstairs in the hall. Dougal picked up the receiver, conscious that both Hanbury and Miss Carrot were hovering within earshot by the open door of the drawing room. He was as curious as they were; no young ladies of his acquaintance knew that he was at the Vineyards. He told the unknown caller that William Dougal was speaking.

There was a sharp intake of breath at the other end of the line—the sort of gasp you made when you were about to undertake something exceptionally strenuous.

"You don't know me," the woman said. "I'm a—a friend of Peter's. Look, can you come round to his—our flat? I know it's a bit—well, I wouldn't ask if it wasn't important."

The voice was jerky with nervousness. The speaker

73

sounded young and frightened. The flat Fen vowels were prominent enough to explain Miss Carrot's unspoken qualification of the word "lady."

Now why on earth, Dougal wondered, *should Sally want to see me?*

Dougal was on foot: the rain had stopped and both he and Sophie were in need of exercise.

Following Hanbury's directions, he walked down River Hill from the marketplace and crossed the river by Bishopsbridge. Here—beyond both the river and the railway—Rosington became a different town, inhabited by people who had nothing to do with the cathedral, the school or the Vineyards.

In the old town, on the hill round the cathedral, the streetplan was medieval and few of the buildings were younger than the century—even the supermarkets tried to disguise their modernity; every lamp-post carried a litter bin and the dogs—with the natural exception of Sophie—seemed far too well-bred to foul the pavements.

But here in this unobtrusively sited suburb, the roads met each other at right angles; the buildings were much younger than the century, though many of them seemed prematurely afflicted with senile decay.

An east wind had sprung up in place of the rain. It blew a sodden crisp packet sluggishly towards them, tempting Sophie to fresh paroxysms of barking. A flotilla of empty cans had collected in the puddle above a blocked drain.

One side of the road was lined with scruffy office blocks, some of which had boarded-up doors and windows. Few of them showed signs of life, for it was well after six o'clock. Opposite them was a line of semi-detached council houses; each pair was separated from its neighbours by precisely the same distance. Only the gardens gave

74

much clue to the character of each household. Some of the houses had obviously passed into private ownership for they sported freshly painted woodwork or neo-Georgian front doors.

Some whim of the architect had placed all the kitchens at the front of the houses. Each of them seemed to contain a tired woman, displaying her domestic abilities to the rest of the world. Televisions chattered through open windows.

Four youths crossed the road and walked beside Dougal. One of them said it was a nice evening; another asked for a light; and a third suggested that Dougal might like to contribute to a charity they were collecting for. Sophie's response was so vigorous that she almost strangled herself against her collar. The youths became aggrieved, rather than aggressive, and eventually decided to look for easier prey.

Dougal scratched Sophie behind the ears until his trembling stopped. He told himself that the trembling was due to the overproduction of adrenalin, rather than to fear, but failed to convince himself.

He walked on to the second set of traffic lights. Hereward Avenue was the turning on the left. It was a section of the Rosington by-pass, and the traffic was consequently much heavier than on the road he had left.

Muir House was on the left-hand side, about a hundred yards from the junction. It was one of four identical blocks of flats set in an undulating sea of landscaped mud, which Dougal identified as the communal garden. The flats themselves looked like baby tower blocks whose growth had been arrested at the fifth storey.

The lift was out of order. Dougal and Sophie climbed the urine-scented stairs to the top floor. The inhabitants had made a spirited attempt to relieve the drabness of the decor. Fascism and football supplied the richest sources of motifs, with sex coming a poor third. Dougal wondered if the artist who had adorned the Morris Traveller was among the exhibitors.

He rang the bell of number 51. He smiled encouragingly at the fish-eye lens of the door's spy-hole. It was perhaps fortunate that the lens' range of vision was unlikely to reach down to the level where Sophie was rootling among the rubbish, like a pig searching for truffles.

Bolts rattled back and the door opened. On the threshold was a plump woman in her early twenties; she had dyed blonde hair; her jeans and shirt clung to her like a wet suit. Her first words were drowned by Sophie's barking.

"Have you any chocolate?" Dougal shouted. "It seems to shut her up."

Sally grasped the essentials of the situation with commendable rapidity. She waved Dougal and Sophie through the small hallway and into the living room; she herself vanished into what appeared to be a kitchen, closing the door behind her.

The room was clean and relatively tidy, despite the fact that the components of a motorcycle filled a third of the available floor space. Humphrey Bogart was mouthing soundless syllables on the big television screen; beneath the set was a video tape recorder, flanked by shelves which held audio equipment and hundreds of tapes and records. A three-piece suite, upholstered in shiny red plastic, was grouped around a large coffee table; its wooden top was scarred with cigarette burns.

The big window faced west. An orange sun trailed veils of blood across the blue haze of the sky. The old town of Rosington had become a sombre celestial city, a place of shadows and fiery outlines. Only that monstrous stone insect in its midst seemed capable of dealing with the sun on equal terms.

Dougal turned away from the window. Humphrey Bogart was lighting a cigarette, which inspired him to do likewise. As he pitched the match into the ashtray, the door opened. Sally came in with a tray bearing two cans of lager, glasses and a jumbo packet of chocolate biscuits.

"Will these do?" she asked.

Dougal nodded. "She goes for quantity rather than quality every time. Do you mind if I feed her here? I'm afraid it's not a pretty sight."

Sophie was proving a positive asset this evening, Dougal thought as the dog bolted down biscuit after biscuit; first she had saved his wallet, and now she was helping both Sally and himself to cope with the initial embarrassment of their meeting.

Sally switched off the television and sat down opposite him.

"I hope that was a tape," Dougal said. "I'd hate to deprive you of the second half of *Casablanca*."

"It's a tape. Anyway, I've seen it about twelve times." A worried expression settled on her round face. "Look, I hope I didn't drag you away from the party."

"I was glad to get away." Dougal wondered where Carrot was. Surely he would have emerged by now if he was in the flat? "Why do you want to see me?"

"Pete isn't here," Sally said in a rush, answering his thoughts rather than his words. "He came back an hour ago. He told me a bit about it, and then he went down the pub with his mates."

And left you behind to worry. Dougal said gently: "I talked to him at the Vineyards."

"I know. He said you were the only person who seemed halfways human. I said, well why don't we talk to you then, but he was too restless; he had to go out."

"The speed?"

Sally looked quickly at him, her expression a curious blend of fear and relief. "Yeah. That and what happened up at the Vineyards. Or what didn't happen. He expected—oh, he can be so stupid sometimes."

For an instant Dougal glimpsed someone else behind the protective screen of make-up: a motherly woman full of fear for her child.

"Did you tell him you were going to ring me?"

She shook her head. "Don't worry—he won't be back until closing-time. And he'll be so pissed he can't stand up."

"It's not that—I just wondered if this was his idea or yours."

"It was mine. Oh God, I don't know what to do. He's going to get violent again—I know the signs. If he's not careful, they're going to lock him up like his grandad."

"They *jailed* Ezekiel Carrot?"

"Nah." Sally took one of Dougal's cigarettes. He lit a match for her. As she bent forward, he caught sight of a plain gold crucifix nestling between her breasts. "They don't put folks like that in jail if they can help it." There was no bitterness in her voice: she was stating a fact of life. "They put him in that loony bin near Charleston Parva. D'you know it? The Burnhams used to live there, years ago. Big old place outside the village. Gives me the creeps."

"Why?"

"He started attacking people on the streets—like hitting them with his stick. He thought everyone was conspiring to kill him. Especially all them vicars. So Peter's aunts had him put away. Not Peter's ma—she was too young." She lowered her voice, as if she feared that the cathedral behind her might hear what she was saying. "They put him in a padded cell, and he hung himself."

The ghost of a mad suicide hovered briefly between

78

them. Dougal swallowed the rest of his lager. He declined Sally's offer of another can.

"Pete's all right when he's with me," she continued. "And he's okay when he's with his mates. I know they do silly things sometimes, but there's no real harm in it. It only gets bad when he sees his family and the rest of the people up the hill. They treat him like a piece of shit, but they won't let him go."

"If I were you, I'd leave Rosington—both of you, I mean. Out of sight and out of mind."

Dougal knew he had said the wrong thing as soon as he had said it. Sally stared at him for a few seconds, her mouth tight with anger.

"I don't want your bloody advice. That's the trouble with you lot—you're always free with advice, aren't you? What makes you think you're so clever? I can find my own answers, thank you very much."

"I'm sorry. I didn't mean to sound patronizing."

Sally's frown dissolved into a grin. "I know you didn't. You think patronizing the proles is a bad habit, and you try not to do it. But sometimes you do it without meaning to."

Dougal grinned. He decided he liked Sally, despite the fact she had the power to make him feel like a six-year-old caught with his hand in mummy's purse. "Now you're patronizing me," he said. "Does that make us quits?"

Sally shrugged. "Some people will never be quits, and you know it." She gave him no time to work out whether she was making a general statement about the class system or simply saying something rather personal about the two of them alone. "I want you to do something for me. Tell them to leave Pete alone."

"Tell who? Look, I hardly know these people. Only James Hanbury."

"The fat smoothie who Pete thinks is his dad? You can

79

tell him for a start. But make sure that his mum and his aunts and all the do-gooders get the message as well. They'll listen to you. You talk the same language."

And that, Dougal realized, was an accusation, not a compliment. "I suppose I can try," he said. "But—"

"If they keep interfering," Sally said in a calm, hard voice, "Pete's going to go over the edge. And if he does that, someone might get killed."

Seven

"A return to Cheltenham, please."

"For God's sake, William!" Hanbury edged Dougal out of the way and peered through the perforated porthole at the ticket clerk. "Make that a first-class return, will you?" He tossed his American Express card on to the clerk's turntable and looked sternly at Dougal. "There's no need to be cheeseparing. It's my money you're spending."

"Sorry. I wasn't thinking."

"And mind you take a taxi to get across London. No piddling around in tubes. And don't forget to have a decent lunch."

Hanbury continued to act like an overprotective nanny as they waited on the platform for the train. Dougal refused to let it irritate him. Hanbury, his confidence restored by his triumphant re-entry into society, was perhaps trying to compensate for the fact that he himself had required a nanny for the last few days. In nursery terms, he was simply getting his own back.

In the distance, Dougal could hear muffled barking. Sophie had sensed that he was deserting her, for a few hours at least, and had already begun to complain about their enforced separation. Hanbury had tried to bribe Dougal into taking Sophie with him; but Dougal had refused. Sophie was Hanbury's problem; he had said this to himself and Hanbury so often in the last few days that he was starting to suspect that it might not be entirely true.

The level-crossing gates at the end of the platform swung across the road. The train was on its way at last.

Hanbury glanced at his watch. "Late as usual," he said. "You will remember that little restaurant near Paddington, won't you? Alfonsin's. Praed Street—you can't miss it. Mention my—"

"James, I should have asked you this before. Where did you go to on the evening that Molly died?"

"Here it is." Hanbury turned away to watch the train as it slid along the platform.

"Where?"

"As a matter of fact"—Hanbury continued to stare at the train—"I went to see Claud Vosper. I did him a good turn once in Cairo. I told Molly where I was going, but not why. I wanted it to be a surprise. Point is, Claud's chairman of the Rosington District Council. I thought Molly would—ah—be rather pleased if I took an interest in local politics."

The newspaper files were cunningly concealed in the basement labyrinth beneath Cheltenham Library. A librarian escorted Dougal down there but left him to find what he wanted by himself.

On every side of him towered huge volumes of yellowing newspaper. It was a sepulchre of ephemera; and Dougal was pleasantly diverted by the thought that he was a tomb-robber. He much preferred to have newspapers mouldering in their original state, rather than preserved on the spurious and inconvenient medium of microfilm.

There were two local newspapers—the *Gloucestershire Echo* and the *Cheltenham Chronicle*. Hanbury had told him the year he wanted, but had been unable to be more precise. Dougal could see no alternative to slogging his way through from January to December.

The *Chronicle* was a weekly, so Dougal began with that. It was a slow process—not so much because of the nature of the job as because of his own inability to resist temptation. He was looking for two words, preferably in conjunction—*Jermyn* and *murder*. But his attention strayed among the forgotten minutiae of other people's lives.

Such was the fascination exerted by the doings of the Women's Institute and the fashion advertisements of the 1950s that Dougal took an hour to reach the end of January. Realizing that at this rate he would have to make an overnight stay, he rationed himself to fifteen minutes for each month. By May his hands were dark with printers' ink.

He struck what he wanted in June. It was such a short item that he nearly missed it. Even the headline—BODY FOUND—was terse to the point of ambiguity.

The body of a man identified as Charles Henry Jermyn was discovered last Friday at a cottage in Pormon. It is understood that the police are pursuing their enquiries.

Dougal leafed on to the next week's edition. This carried a brief report of the coroner's inquest.

But it did contain some useful information. Jermyn, who was described as a gardener, had been discovered by his employer, Dr. Richard Fleetwood, in the kitchen of his cottage. He had been strangled. The pathologist put the time of death as somewhere between three or four weeks before the discovery of the corpse. The police were still pursuing their enquiries. The verdict was murder by person or persons unknown. The coroner made a few remarks about the dangers of allowing vagrants into one's home. Nothing that Dougal could find in the rest of the report lent substance to this comment.

He moved on to the *Echo*. Several issues touched on the Jermyn murder, but the reporting was as laconic as the *Chronicle*'s had been.

Dougal frowned. He walked round the labyrinth to find out what else it contained. *The Times* was available, so he tried that. The case wasn't even mentioned.

The two volumes containing the *Echo* and the *Chronicle* were still on the table. Dougal pulled out a spiral-bound shorthand pad from his briefcase and copied out the relevant extracts. He stared at his own writing while his biro, apparently of its own accord, doodled busily beneath it. The doodle turned into an ornate question mark.

He tapped the doodle with the tip of his biro and added two more question marks, one on either side of the original; this time the design was severely functional.

There were three questions. Unless he could find the answers, his journey would have been wasted.

He spent the next half-hour prowling round the reference library upstairs. Pormon, he discovered from a gazetteer, was a village eight miles south-west of Cheltenham; its population had been 562 at the last count; and the vicar was the Reverend George Telfer.

The Medical Register was the next step. Dr. Richard Fleetwood was not listed. That meant he was dead, disbarred or not a doctor of medicine at all. Dougal resolutely closed his mind to all the other possibilities; the trouble with keeping an open mind was that everything flooded into it.

He needed facts, not speculations. A methodical search

through the obvious sources must come first. What he wanted was not on the open shelves, so he joined the queue which straggled up to the counter.

There was an irritating delay before he was served. It was lunchtime, he realized; and the counter was understaffed in consequence. He asked for the Voters' List and retired with his prize to a quiet corner near the photocopying machine.

Fate rewarded his persistence. The name of Fleetwood leapt up at him as he scanned the enfranchised inhabitants of Pormon. There were two of them—Herbert Richard and Magdalene Mary. Their address was given as Mannering House.

The next step was to cross-check the information with the telephone directory. Here he ran into a snag: neither of the Fleetwoods was listed. But that in itself might be significant.

He collated the scraps of information: the title of doctor; an address which lacked the vulgar identification of a house number; a telephone number—assuming there was one—which was ex-directory; a garden which must be reasonably spacious if it had required a gardener; and of course a financial position which permitted the employment of a gardener, albeit in the 1950s. Taken together, these facts suggested that Herbert Richard was one of Pormon's more solid citizens.

He glanced at his watch: time was creeping on, and he wanted some lunch. A twinge of guilt assailed him: a dedicated researcher would stay in the library and continue to quarry after truth. There was at least a chance that he might be able to discover more about the Fleetwoods—solid citizens tended to leave more traces of their passage through life in the written word than their less substantial brethren. For example, it might be instructive to return to the labyrinth and plough through

The Times index; or he could investigate the countless professional directories around the walls of the reference library. Alternatively, he might visit the local newspaper offices.

But the needs of the flesh outweighed the duties of the spirit. Dougal did make one concession to the latter, however: on his way out, he tried *Who's Who*.

To his great relief, he found that FLEETWOOD, Herbert Richard, had earned an entry. The man turned out to be a physicist who had spent most of his adult life in universities, apart from four years with the RAF during the war. He was sixty-six and had retired last year; he was now an emeritus professor of the University of Bristol. The titles of his publications were largely incomprehensible to Dougal. He was a widower who admitted to one daughter. He had no clubs; if he had any recreations he preferred to keep them to himself.

Discretion seemed to be Fleetwood's watchword. It was a bad omen.

It sounded as though someone was dragging a heavy weight across the floor on the other side of the door.

Dougal kept his imagination on a tight rein. There was no reason whatsoever why the heavy weight should be a corpse. But Mannering House and its environs encouraged fancies like this, even on a summer afternoon.

The house was half a mile outside the village, screened from the road by a line of ragged yews. It was a detached Victorian villa with windows which were too large for its façade. The house had been rendered at some point in its history; and the perpetrator had compounded this by scratching rectangles over the smooth surface, presumably to give the illusion that the building was faced with dressed stone. Worst of all, the outside walls had been painted dark red; the paint had now weathered to the color a joint of beef acquired when it had stayed too long in the butcher's window.

The black front door swung inwards. A small woman, supported by two aluminum crutches, stared at him without speaking.

Dougal hoped the pity wasn't showing in his face. "Is Professor Fleetwood in?" The words came out more abruptly than he had intended; he tried to soften them with a smile.

"He's in London." There was no answering smile.

In other circumstances, the face would have been beautiful and the body beneath it voluptuous. But the face was tight with strain, as if the woman's teeth were usually clenched; the skinny legs, both encased in irons, made a mockery of the full breasts; the shoulders were heavy beneath her sleeveless cotton dress.

"Are you Miss Fleetwood? My name's William Dougal."

She nodded. Her muscular arms tightened round the crutches.

"I'm sorry to trouble you. A cousin of mine once worked for your father. I wanted to ask Professor Fleetwood a few questions about him. His name was Charles Jermyn."

The suspicion and the tension on Magdalene Fleetwood's face was briefly overlaid by another, softer expression. Dougal realized with a shock that it was pity—and that the pity was directed at him.

"You'd better come in."

She manoeuvred herself backwards into the hall. Dougal followed her in and closed the door behind him. The hall was a large, clean box, without any furniture whatsoever.

"In there," she said, pointing with her head towards a door on the left.

Dougal preceded her, guessing that she preferred to

move at her own pace and unobserved. He found himself in a high-ceilinged drawing room with a marble fireplace, on either side of which was a chintz-covered sofa. There were plenty of bookcases but no television. It was cool in here, despite the warmth of the day.

She followed him into the room and lowered herself on to one of the sofas. She rested her crutches against the arm. One of them slid sideways on to the carpet. Dougal retrieved it and returned it to its original position. She didn't say thank you. She must have had ample time to get tired of thanking people.

"Won't you sit down, Mr. Dougal?" Now she was seated, some of the strain had left her low-pitched voice. "I thought Charles didn't have any relatives in this country?"

Charles?

"My mother was his second cousin once removed. We came back to England in the sixties—I was born in Australia." Dougal noticed there were two romantic novels half concealed beneath the bundle of knitting beside Magdalene. "To tell the truth, I'd never even heard of Charles Jermyn until very recently. My mother had lost touch with him completely before he died. But I started tracing our family tree—and there he was."

She closed her eyes for an instant, as if shutting him out. "You know what happened to him?"

"I know he was strangled—that was on the death certificate."

"But how did you get my father's name?"

"He was mentioned in the report in the *Echo*. I spent the morning in Cheltenham Library, going through their back issues."

"You're going to a lot of trouble." Her hands coiled round each other on her lap; the knuckles whitened.

Dougal shrugged. "I was curious. Charles is the only

genuine skeleton in my family's cupboard. We're a boring lot. It seems a shame that no one should remember him."

"*I* remember him," Magdalene said abruptly. "I always will."

"But you must have been very young—"

"I was five. But Charles was my . . . friend."

Dougal realized that he had unwittingly blundered into an emotional minefield. Curiosity fought a quick duel with good manners; and for once good manners won.

"Look, I'm sorry—I don't want to dig up unhappy memories. And I'm taking up your time. I can always write to Professor Fleetwood."

Magdalene shook her head. "Don't go. I don't mind talking about Charles. In fact it's rather nice—my father never mentions him." She forced a smile. "Besides, I don't want Charles to be forgotten. Ask whatever you want."

"If you're sure." Dougal gave her a few seconds to change her mind. What role did Charles Jermyn play in her memories, he wondered—a knight on a white charger who died before he could rescue her? "First of all, it seemed strange that he should be working here. How did that happen?"

"Strange because he'd been to a public school?" Magdalene's hands relaxed. "Not really. I think he was at a loose end. He had no immediate family to tell him what to do. He turned up on the doorstep in spring, asking if there was any work he could do. My father had just sacked our old gardener and the garden was in a mess. That's how it started."

There was a wide, trusting smile on Magdalene's face. It wasn't directed at Dougal but at the ghost of Charles Jermyn. Dougal squirmed inwardly. Since this invisible third party had joined them, he himself was in the way; he felt like an eavesdropper.

89

Now she had started to talk, the only problem was channelling the flow. Magdalene leant forward, her face intent; the words spilled out of her as if they had been waiting to be spoken for far too long. Dougal groped for the reality which lay behind the recalled perceptions of a five-year-old—and behind what he suspected was the distortion of thirty years of fantasy.

Jermyn, it seemed, had been living rough for a month or two before his arrival at Mannering House. He had fallen out of the tightly organized routine of school life and found nothing to take its place. Magdalene hinted that he was haunted by a dark secret; but Dougal thought that might be an accretion which had been suggested by the books she read.

The Fleetwood family had taken to him from the first. He was a hard-working gardener; and Magdalene's father—who seemed, reading between the lines, to be distinctly eccentric where human relationships were concerned—had taken a liking to him. Fleetwood offered him a permanent job—and somewhere to live; there was a semi-derelict cottage at the far end of the garden.

Jermyn had played with Magdalene and occasionally babysat while her parents were out.

"My mother was alive then. She died in a car crash when I was eleven. There's a picture of her over there."

Dougal stood up to examine the photograph on the end of the mantelpiece. It showed what nature had had in mind when it designed Magdalene Fleetwood—before polio, perhaps, had modified the plan. Her mother had been a dark-haired, shapely woman with a smile which could only be described as roguish. Beside her towered a thin-lipped man in baggy shorts and sandals; he looked at least ten years older than she; he was frowning at the camera. The contrast between them started another train of thought in Dougal's mind: perhaps Mrs. Fleetwood

90

had also taken a liking to Charles Jermyn.

Jermyn had settled quickly into his new life. He had sent for his belongings, which were apparently confined to the contents of a couple of trunks, and made the cottage as habitable as possible. Dougal asked if he had got to know anyone else in the village.

Magdalene shook her head. "We've never had much to do with the people in Pormon." She made it sound like a virtue. "And it's only since Daddy retired that we've been here all the year round. The villagers aren't very welcoming at the best of times. You have to be born in Pormon to belong to it. I suppose Charles must have shopped there sometimes. But I know he used to go into Cheltenham on his days off."

She implied that Jermyn had not needed any other company. A welter of memories emerged: Jermyn telling her a bedtime story about a ghost in an old church; Jermyn helping Mrs. Fleetwood sort the wools for her embroidery, while Magdalene crawled adoringly around them; Jermyn climbing the oak tree at the bottom of the garden to rescue a kitten with no head for heights. Jermyn, in fact, seemed little short of a youthful Sir Galahad.

Dougal steered her back to what he hoped was the point. "If he was so much part of the family, why was it three or four weeks before his body was found?"

Magdalene screwed up her face like an unwanted piece of paper. When her muscles relaxed, her expression was bleak. Dougal swore at himself for having been so crass.

"It was termtime. Daddy was at Oxford then. We had a flat off the Banbury Road."

"And Charles stayed in the cottage and looked after the garden?"

She nodded. "He kept an eye on the house as well. Sometimes we came down at the weekends. But my father was very busy—we didn't get down for the last four

91

weekends of that Trinity term. I last saw Charles on May the twenty-third."

"Did they ever find out who—who was responsible?"

"No." She brought her clenched fist down on the knitting. "I wish they had! I wish they'd hanged him. There was a tramp in the area, but they never traced him."

"Was anything missing?"

"No one really knew. There was no money in the house. Not much food, either. The kitchen window catch was broken. They thought the tramp must have broken in while Charles was out. Then Charles came back and the tramp . . . the tramp . . ."

"Yes, I see. I suppose he must have left fingerprints?"

Magdalene seized upon the diversion: "They found five different lots—Charles's, of course, mine, my parents' and someone else's. At least that's what my father told me afterwards."

"They didn't mention that in the papers. In fact they didn't mention very much at all."

"My father doesn't encourage snoopers."

Her voice was cold, and Dougal realized that he had to be cautious. At present he was acceptable to her—as a cousin of Jermyn's and as a temporary relief from loneliness and tedium. But one false move could topple him from this favoured position.

"I imagine the police wouldn't encourage them either," he said lightly. "Not while the investigation was in progress. It must have been a great shock to your father when he found Charles—"

"*I* was the first to find him," Magdalene interrupted. "My father told the police that he had, because he didn't want me being badgered with questions. But it was me, I tell you."

She leant towards him, her face slightly flushed, as if imploring him to believe her.

"It's a long time ago," Dougal frowned. "Are you *sure*?"

"Of course I am," she snapped back. "It's not something you imagine. As soon as we got home I wanted to see Charles. So I ran down the garden—"

Dougal's expression made her break off abruptly. The flush deepened. She scowled at him. "It was later that summer I got polio. Before that, I was just like anybody else."

"I'm sorry."

Magdalene waved his apology aside. "The door was locked, but I knew where he kept the key. There was this awful smell when I opened the door. He was on the floor by the sink. All swollen and discoloured. He . . . he didn't look like a human at all. I didn't realize it was him. Not until I saw the tie."

"What tie?" Dougal guessed the answer even as he asked the question.

"It was what the killer used. Charles used to wear it in the evenings occasionally. It was silk—I can remember the feel of it. It had pink and silver stripes."

Eight

Dougal walked between rank, untrimmed hedgerows, back to the centre of Pormon. He was hot, dusty, and unusually depressed. He felt contaminated by despair.

Most of the village was grouped round an intersection where three roads met. The little streets were empty. The pub was closed, owing to the absurdities of England's licensing laws. So were the three shops. Finding a drink of any sort was out of the question. Dougal would have settled for a can of something sweet and fizzy, as long as it was cold.

There was a telephone box on a triangular patch of scrubby grass between two of the roads. Dougal found the taxis in the Yellow Pages and ordered a mini-cab. The despatcher promised it would be there within twenty minutes. It sounded like one of those promises which are made to be broken.

Dougal pushed open the door of the phone box to let in some air. Half-formed suspicions were floating in his mind; they were restless and indestructible, like the dreams which flourished during a fever. He tried to ignore them for the moment by concentrating on his three questions. Magdalene had provided plausible answers for two of them—the delay in finding Jermyn's body and the cursory coverage of the murder in the local press.

Plausible—but not necessarily truthful.

The third question—the identity of the killer—remained unanswered; from this question dangled a subsidiary one—did Jermyn's death have anything to do with Molly Burnham's?

It occurred to him that there was a chance he might be able to prove or disprove one of his suspicions today. He picked up the alphabetical directory and found another telephone number and the address which went with it.

A few minutes later, he crossed the road to wait for the taxi in the relative cool of the church porch. Why was it, he wondered, that nourishing suspicions of other people always made him suspicious of his own motives? He was beginning to question whether he had taken this on to *help* Hanbury. The risks associated with touching pitch ran uneasily through his mind as he waited.

Thirty minutes later, a large, dented saloon pulled up at the gate to the churchyard. Dougal climbed in.

"You want Cheltenham station," the driver told him. Like his car, he was large, dented and smelt of stale beer.

"No I don't," Dougal snapped. "I want an off-licence. Then I want to go to Ashton Avenue in Gloucester."

"Suit yourself, guv. It's a free country. Never be afraid to change your mind, that's what I say. But it'll cost you another fiver. It's further, see?"

During the drive, Dougal stonewalled the driver's attempts to share his homespun philosophy. At the off-licence, a series of choices confronted him. He selected a half-bottle of brandy and a half of whisky. It was never easy to cater for other people's vices. He also brought a small carton of orange juice to drink in the taxi.

Ashton Avenue was a quiet, broad road in the northern outskirts of Gloucester. The trees were large and old; the houses were large and modern. Children, Dougal felt, instinctively lowered their voices here; even the traffic sounded subdued.

The Sunnyvale Complex was a four-storey block of flats which ran round three sides of a forecourt. It was set in a small but tastefully manicured garden. People were having tea in the garden and on some of the balconies. All of them were old.

The foyer had piped music and a jungle of pot-plants. Every attempt had been made to conceal the medical infrastructure which supported, like a skeleton beneath the flesh, the determined and healthy normality of the complex. It was the sort of place where ambulances and undertakers used the tradesmen's entrance. The comfortable chairs, the brightly painted sign to the recreation rooms and the smile on the receptionist's face all had the same subliminal message: you came here to enjoy yourself, not to die.

The receptionist, whose voice he recognized from the telephone, directed him to Charles Hanbury's flat on the second floor.

"Just ring the bell and wait." Her eyelashes fluttered. "He's quite a mobile old boy."

Charles Hanbury greeted Dougal with an enthusiasm which verged on the morbid; it suggested that guests were so rare that he was quite prepared to eat them in order to keep them with him for longer. He shuffled in front of Dougal through the hall to his crowded sitting room. He moved slowly, with the aid of a stick, but neither the wheelchair nor the attendant nurse was in evidence; perhaps they were needed only when Hanbury ventured into the outside world. The old man was taller than he had seemed in the wheelchair.

"Very civil of you to ring. Very civil. Just passing

96

through, eh? Always delighted to see any friend of James's. How is he? How's Molly?"

Dougal, uncertain whether Charles Hanbury had never heard of Molly's death, or had merely forgotten about it, replied that they seemed to have enjoyed their honeymoon.

"Good, good. They sent me a postcard. Do sit down, my dear fellow. I'll pour the tea."

A tea tray was already waiting on the table between the two armchairs. As Dougal put down his briefcase beside his chair, the two bottles it contained clanked together. Hanbury's eyes narrowed.

"I do wish I could offer you a snifter with this. Tea's such an insipid drink by itself. Loathe the stuff myself."

"As it happens," Dougal said.

There was no need to say more. The old man hid the brandy in his bookcase, behind a leather-bound set of Dickens' novels; to be precise, it was behind *Great Expectations* and *Our Mutual Friend*. He poured an inch of the whisky into Dougal's cup, before the latter could prevent him, and rather more into his own. He concealed the bottle itself between the arm and the seat of the chair.

"Sorry about that, old chap." He sank back in his chair and added tea and milk to both cups. The tea was so stewed it was almost black. "The people here can be so childish about one's little pleasures. Between you and me, most of them are tiresome killjoys. Cheers."

In the event Dougal was glad of the whisky: the tea was not only stewed, it was cold. Charles Hanbury announced proudly that he had made it himself when he knew Dougal was coming.

When the old man was on his second cup of fortified tea, Dougal tried to lead the conversation away from the iniquities of the Sunnyvale Complex and towards James

Hanbury. This proved unexpectedly difficult. Charles Hanbury was full of venom and rarely had a chance to offload it. His main, and constantly reiterated, criticism of the people whom he referred to as "my blasted gaolers" was that they treated him like a forgetful and incapable child.

"And that's ridiculous," he said. "My memory's as good as theirs. Better, in fact. That's legal training for you."

Dougal discarded finesse. "Could you tell me, for example, where James was, thirty years ago?"

"Pa! Of course I could. Why should I, though? *I* know I know, and that's the main thing. And if necessary I can provide written evidence to prove it. Always have it in writing: that's my advice to you, young man."

"You keep a record of everything that happens to you? A diary?"

Charles Hanbury shook his head. "Scribblings after the event don't constitute objective evidence. Diaries are a form of self-indulgence. Almost as bad as that fellow Proust and his bloody madeleine. Can't get much more subjective than that."

The old man's disgust brought on a fit of coughing. Dougal began to doubt the wisdom of his visit: it had never been more than a long shot at a target which might not even be there in the first place. But obstinacy forced him onwards.

"Letters?" he said. "Account books, theatre programmes—that sort of thing?"

Hanbury wiped his nose, mouth and eyes with a large grubby handkerchief. "See those cupboards?" He waved his handkerchief over his shoulder. Behind him was a row of bookcases with cupboards built into their bases. "It's all there—in box files. Well, actually some of it's in the bedroom and some of it's in store. Don't have the

98

space now. But when I die, they won't be able to pretend I didn't exist. Oh no. I'd stand up in a court of law."

Dougal had a vision of a mound of box files, seven feet high and laced with pink ribbons; they were arranged as precisely as possible around the contours of Charles Hanbury; and when the old man died, the centre of the pile would contain nothing but the absence of a body, like a discarded snail shell.

The conversation—or rather Hanbury's monologue—rambled on for another thirty minutes. During this time, most of the whisky was consumed. Hanbury forgot about his archives; instead he described a scheme for bringing a civil action against the company which owned the Sunnyvale Complex. He repeated it twice, with minor variations each time. Dougal, shackled by his obligations as a guest and by a growing sense of guilt, remained a prisoner in his chair, distributing approving nods and grunts when his host gave him the cue. He wondered, not for the first time, why these ancient mariners who so frequently buttonholed him never realized, the monotony of his responses, that he was bored. Perhaps there were two types of ancient mariner: a lesser breed which recognized the tedium it generated but was forced to suppress the knowledge because of its paramount need to bore; and a superior race of dedicated bores whose belief in their ability to fascinate others was unshakeable. Charles Hanbury fell into the second category of Absolute Bore.

But even as he talked and drank, a change was taking place in the old man. The animation gradually drained away; he began to slur his words; his sentences became fragmentary, as if he was articulating only part of what he was saying in his mind.

His head bobbed down, so that the chin was resting on the chest, and then jerked back to the vertical. This happened twice more; it had no discernible effect on the trickle of words. But on the fourth occasion, the chin stayed where it had fallen. The mouth hung open; false teeth sparkled youthfully against old, blotched skin.

Papery eyelids, networked with veins, obscured Hanbury's astonishingly blue eyes. The breathing grew heavier; it modulated from wheezing to snoring. The rasp of air was the only sound in the stuffy room.

The chair creaked as Dougal stood up. He tiptoed across the carpet, pausing to listen at every step. The rhythm of the snores had a soothing, almost hypnotic quality. Charles Hanbury was now invisible behind the high back of his armchair. By the same token, should he open his eyes, he would not see Dougal. Old people often slept lightly.

Dougal refused to give himself time to think; if he did so, he would disapprove of what he was doing. The cupboard beneath the collected works of Dickens was the nearest. The door's hinges screeched as he started to pull it open. He counted to ten, straining to catch the slightest alteration in Hanbury's breathing.

Crouching down on his haunches, he peered into the gap between the edge of the door and its frame. There were two shelves inside, on each of which were three rows of dusty glasses. He pushed the door shut, reducing the screech to a whisper.

Practice made his movements swifter. He investigated the other three cupboards. One contained nothing but empty decanters, some without stoppers and many of them chipped and stained; they were the neglected memorials of a lifetime's dissipation. The next cupboard was devoted to colour supplements from the Sunday newspapers. The third was empty.

Dougal slipped into the hall. One door led to a walk-in cupboard: it held overcoats, a surprising number of umbrellas and, propped against one wall and folded, the wheelchair which the old man had used at the wedding.

The doors to the kitchen and the bathroom were ajar. They were tiny rooms with no secrets. The bedroom briefly revived Dougal's hopes. It was an invalid's room, with an emergency bell wired into the wall above the night table and a walking frame beside the bed. Dougal investigated the built-in wardrobe and the cupboard above it; but neither of them held box files.

It was possible that the Hanbury archives were fabulous creations, like the great libraries of Atlantis; they might be no more than an imagined by-product of a lifetime's involvement with litigation and alcohol. Charles Hanbury based his claim to exist on these files: if they didn't exist, then—logically if absurdly—nor did he.

Dougal's eyes idly raked along the bottom of the wardrobe. The floor-space was filled with clutter: rusting golf clubs stacked drunkenly in one corner, a trouser press of considerable antiquity, a jumble of shoes and a chamberpot. The clothes above were a drab collection: black, navy-blue and dark grey. But there was one splash of colour, partly obscured by the golf clubs. It was the last colour Dougal would have expected to find in the old man's wardrobe—a gay, almost lurid pink.

A pink ribbon.

He lifted away two of the golf clubs. There were two pink ribbons; each girdled a bulging shoe box. He lifted them out of the wardrobe. It was easier to slide the ribbons lengthways of the boxes rather than to undo the knots. Dust smudged his fingers: no one had touched these boxes for years.

Both of them contained letters, still in their original envelopes and filed upright like index cards. He pulled out half a dozen at random, three from each box. They were all addressed to Charles Hanbury: so he did exist, or at least used to do so, after all.

Judging by the postmarks, the letters had been filed in chronological order. The contents in the first box belonged to the 1930s and the reign of George V. The handwriting on the envelopes was unfamiliar—love letters, perhaps from Charles's wife and James's mother? Dougal hastily pushed them back in their box, replaced the ribbon and thrust the box among the golf clubs.

The letters in the second box were twenty years later in date. Dougal flicked through them, glancing at the postmarks. The great majority of them had been franked in Rosington. All of them were addressed in a sprawling hand which, as the years passed, grew florid and assured; but it still sprawled across the envelopes.

James Hanbury's handwriting had changed very little since his teens.

Panic bubbled up inside Dougal. He glanced at the doorway, half afraid that he would find a miraculously mobile and justifiably angry Charles Hanbury glowering down at him. He stuffed about a tenth of the letters into the two side pockets of his jacket. They should cover the dates in which he was interested; he had no desire to linger and make sure. He bundled the box back among the golf clubs and closed the wardrobe door.

On his way back to the sitting room he visited the bathroom, partly from physical necessity and partly to provide himself with an alibi. The flushing of the lavatory took him by surprise: in his present state it sounded like a miniature Niagara.

He needn't have bothered: Charles Hanbury was still in precisely the same position. The snores had modulated back to wheezes. The whisky bottle, with an inch of liquid in the bottom, still stood beside his teacup.

Dougal knew that good manners required him to leave at least a note of farewell. But what could he say? *Must rush. Thank you so much for tea. Have violated your privacy and stolen a few of your son's letters.*

He balked at this, knowing that if he was going to balk at anything he should have done it long ago. He recapped the whisky bottle and stowed it away behind *The Uncommercial Traveller* and *A Tale of Two Cities.*

The old man stirred. His lips smacked together as he closed his mouth. But within seconds the mouth was open again. The chin rose and fell in time with the chest which supported it.

As quietly as possible, Dougal slipped out of the room.

At Paddington, Dougal walked in what was very nearly a straight line across the concourse to the bar. In this station, names and the objects to which they referred often bore little relation to each other: in the concourse was an area called the Green, where no blade of grass had grown for at least a century; the bar was inexplicably named the Knights and Heralds. The anomalies seemed appropriate: William Dougal didn't sound the right name for a seedy little snooper.

He bought a pint and drank it standing at the bar. The beer swiftly glided down; he had already blazed a trail for it in the buffet of the train. He ordered another and glanced around at his fellow drinkers.

Most pubs catered for a homogeneous clientele; you could usually work out the common social, professional or geographical denominator. But the Knights and Heralds was a watering hole for transients. Dowagers from the Shires sipped gins-and-tonic, sheltered by an embankment of Selfridge's bags from red-faced postmen snatching a couple of quick ones between trains; grizzled executives swopped yarns of sexual prowess, usually set in Birmingham; lovers loved one another with their eyes;

loners read or peeped at their neighbours; adolescents poured money into the juke box and the video games.

And they were all strangers who wished they were somewhere else.

Dougal took the second pint to a vacant place on one of the padded horseshoe seats. He needed to make a decision: was he going back to Rosington and his contractual obligations, or was he going home to Kilburn to be himself again?

Furtive curiosity persuaded him to postpone the decision. He opened his briefcase and took out the letters. Somehow he hadn't been able to face them on the train. He sorted them into two piles.

In the first heap were half a dozen letters which dated from the last term of Hanbury's career as a schoolboy. Dougal had written letters like this himself: you wrote them during letter prep after chapel on Sundays; they were compulsory weekly bulletins to your parents. During termtime in the enclosed world of a boarding school, your home life became an abstraction: as a result, your letters tended to become mechanical exercises, addressed to people who seemed only slightly more real than Martians or Venusians.

Hanbury's letters to his father fell into the familiar pattern. They opened with a cursory round-up of the school's news: *The First XI played King's, Ely, away yesterday. We lost by five wickets. I made 8; Pantry wants me to play Mercutio in the school play.* At their close, however, they became thinly veiled begging letters: *Have had to fork out unexpectedly for the Lit. Soc. sub and annual dinner. Would it be possible to have an advance on my holiday allowance? Perhaps £5? Even a pound would help; or, more subtly; Secondhand motorbikes are really very cheap. Frank's parents have promised him one as a leaving present, and I think Tom's have as well.*

104

Two of the letters had been written after Hanbury's escapade in the cathedral, but no mention was made of it. The obvious inference was that the school authorities had been so anxious to cover up the scandal that they hadn't even mentioned it to Charles Hanbury. As far as Dougal was concerned, this avenue of investigation had turned into a cul-de-sac.

The second pile contained a selection of letters written while Hanbury was doing his stint in the army, just after he had left school. They lacked the regularity and frequency of the earlier letters, but one feature remained the same: *It's alarmingly easy to run up bills here. One has to keep up with the other chaps. I wonder if you could tide me over until payday . . .*

In the year of Jermyn's death, Hanbury had been abroad with the British Army of the Rhine. Dougal felt unexpectedly relieved. He celebrated by buying himself another pint. But the next letter he read made the beer more of a consolation than a celebration.

It was dated 15 May. *Will be back in England on the 20th for two or three weeks. They wanted volunteers for a course at Camberley & I volunteered like a shot. I hope to wangle a spot of leave while I'm there—will pop down & see you, if I can.*

The tone of the next letter, five weeks later, was decidedly defensive: *Terribly sorry I couldn't get down to see you. I could only get a couple of days off, and I ran into an old school friend in Town. You know how it is . . .*

Dougal assembled the pieces in his mind: Hanbury had been in England at a time when he claimed to have been abroad; he had met an old school friend; Jermyn had been killed in the last week of May; Hanbury had been known to use a garrotte in the more recent past; Jermyn had pipped Hanbury to the post with Alison and might have taunted Hanbury with his impotence.

It was difficult to imagine Hanbury as the perpetrator

of a crime of passion. On the other hand, it was naïve to suppose that the youthful Hanbury was necessarily guided by the same hardheaded principles of profit and loss that guided him in his maturity, thirty years later.

The beer went sour on him. Dougal pushed aside his glass and glanced at his watch. He had had enough of being a transient, he decided.

It was time to go home.

On a warm summer evening, Kilburn sounded and smelt like a foreign city. Dougal wondered if you could get Guinness and sweet potatoes in Samarkand.

On his way from the bus stop to the flat, he bought a take-away kebab. He promised himself a treat: he would ring Celia this evening. Celia had been his first girlfriend; and now, after a ten year gap in their relationship and the death of her father, she and Dougal were starting to get to know one another again. Dougal was terrified of crowding her into something she might later regret; at present she was vulnerable; and telephoning her out of the blue might be construed, by himself at least, as a selfish luxury. But he needed to talk to her, if only to be reassured that there was life beyond Rosington, and that greed and need were not the only constituents of the social glue which bound people together.

As he put his key in the door, he could hear the phone ringing inside. A jolt of emotion went through him, affecting him like a mild electric shock. *It's Celia.* He burst into the flat, dropped his briefcase and dived for the phone. When he said hello into the mouthpiece, he was embarrassed to hear that it came out as a hoarse whisper.

"William, for God's sake, where have you been? Why aren't you back here? Why haven't you rung?"

Dougal's excitement melted into a puddle of disappointment.

"I don't think there's much point in me coming back to Rosington," he said harshly. "In any case, I need a breathing space. I'll ring you tomorrow."

"But you'll have to come back." Hanbury's voice was calmer now; there was even a hint of amusement in it. "I imagine the police will want to interview you."

"Why should they want to do that?" Dougal instantaneously reviewed his recent activities in Rosington: surely none of them had been criminal?

"Alison was murdered last night."

Nine

Dougal reached Rosington by the last train of the evening. The journey took twice as long as it had done that morning; it involved changing trains and a long delay at Cambridge, where the buffet, of course, was closed.

Hanbury was waiting for him on the platform, with Sophie straining at his side. The dog flung herself on Dougal and dribbled ecstatically over as much of him as she could reach.

"She insisted on coming," Hanbury said. "You've got a friend for life."

As they left the station, Dougal noticed two men examining the timetable on the wall beside the ticket collector's empty kiosk. Sophie tried to sniff their shoes, possibly as a prelude to leaving her canine signature on them. Dougal, using both hands on the lead, dragged her into the car park. He glanced back at them as he and Hanbury walked over to the Range Rover.

Hanbury, with that alarming intuition which he occasionally displayed, seemed to guess what Dougal was thinking. "Quite possibly, I should think."

"The police are playing this one very much by the book. I expect you can guess why."

Dougal said he wasn't in the mood for playing guessing games.

"There may be—ah—international ramifications, you see." Hanbury climbed into the driver's seat and started the engine. "The local chaps may have to account to the NCB at Scotland Yard. The Sûreté—even Interpol—could show an interest. The local chaps are naturally a little jumpy. So of course they put a watch on the station. Damn silly, really."

The Range Rover purred up the hill. The sky still had a trace of daylight; it was a soft, deep blue. A fat orange moon had risen in the east; it looked like a sun which had lost its heat and lost its way. There was little traffic and few pedestrians. A police car passed them, travelling in the opposite direction. The city might have imposed a curfew on itself.

There was a light in an upper-floor window of Pantry's house at the top of the hill. They drove on past the Porta, its great gates barred against the world, and into Minster Street.

"So the police meant nothing personal?"

"I didn't say that." Hanbury glanced into the rear mirror. "I'm not sure." He slowed down for the traffic lights by the Crossed Keys Hotel. They changed to green as he approached but, instead of turning left for Charleston Parva, he drove straight on. "The news only broke this afternoon. Evelyn Pantry phoned me. All he knew was that Alison had been found dead on Plum Hill; strangled, he said. He wouldn't divulge his sources."

They were now in a part of town where Dougal had never been before. Like the suburb beyond the river, it was modern; but there the resemblance ended. This wasn't the sort of place where you dropped litter or built council flats.

Hanbury turned into a side road where the houses were

even larger. "Anything useful come out of your trip to Cheltenham?"

"A few facts. I don't know whether they'll be useful or not. James, where are we going?"

"I thought we'd drop in on Claud Vosper. He may have heard a few more details. Our Claud has an enviable range of contacts."

"Isn't it rather late?"

"He won't mind." Hanbury chuckled. "He gives a lot of people the rough side of his tongue, but not me. Not since Cairo."

Vosper's home was called Manderley. It was shielded from the road by a box hedge and a screen of firs. The house itself was long, low and modern. A wrought-iron balcony ran the length of the first floor. On one side a lawn stretched away until it lost itself in the darkness; on the other, coloured bulbs swayed in the breeze above a swimming pool. There was a BMW parked beside a circular fishpond. A cast-iron cherub urinated into the lilies.

The bell chimed the first five notes of "Oranges and Lemons." The door was opened by an elderly and emaciated blonde; she had a drink in one hand and was trying to restrain an Alsatian with the other. In the background, Sophie barked continuously from the security of the Range Rover.

"Glenys," Hanbury purred. "May we come in? You look positively svelte this evening."

Glenys said nothing but she stood aside to allow them to enter. As soon as Dougal closed the door, the Alsatian lost interest in Sophie and padded away.

"Sorry to disturb you at this hour. Just wanted a quick word with Claud. Is he in the—ah—study?"

Glenys nodded. She swallowed the rest of her drink, muttered something indistinguishable and followed the Alsatian into what looked like a dimly lit sitting room.

Hanbury touched Dougal's arm. "This way." They turned into a passage which led in the general direction of the swimming pool. "Rather sad, really," he said quietly. "Glenys is one of those wives who don't know what to do with themselves when their husbands strike it rich; drink problem, I believe."

He tapped on a leather-covered door, and, without waiting for a reply, went in. In the room beyond was a full-sized billiards table, an immense juke box which was about the same age as Dougal, and a bar. A fat man in a dinner jacket was perched on one of the four bar stools; he was watching "Match of the Day" on a television set which was mounted at eye level on the wall to the right of the bar.

"I'm busy," he said without turning his head. An inch of ash fell from his cigar and lost itself in his ruffled shirt front.

"Aren't we all?" Hanbury crossed the room and switched off the television. "I shan't keep you long. I just want a little information."

Vosper eased himself off the stool. "Any time, James. You know me: always at your service. Can I get you and your friend a drink?" His small, slate-coloured eyes slid across to Dougal and then back to Hanbury.

"Not for me, thank you. By the way, this is my friend and colleague, William Dougal."

"Pleased to meet any friend of James's." Vosper's handshake was as manly as you could get, if you equated manliness with firmness of grip. "Would you like a drink?"

Dougal shook his head. He put his hands behind his back so that he could massage the one which had been injured without causing offence. He had winced, of course, but he hoped he had covered that up with a smile.

Hanbury clambered on to one of the stools and lit a Caporal. "I hear poor Alison Carrot was killed. She was

111

an old friend, you know. The details haven't filtered through to the general public, but I wondered if you might have picked up something."

Vosper scratched his thigh. "I used to know her too," he said. "Remember the old days? Down the Black Pig? Christ, she was a *goer!*"

Something in his voice made Dougal want to look away. He glanced at the juke box. An illuminated couple were doing a frozen hand-jive on its side. You could have three selections for only five cents. All the records were at least a quarter of a century old. He looked at the labels: Bill Haley, Elvis Presley, Jerry Lee Lewis, Chuck Berry: Vosper liked his rock and roll.

"I remember." Hanbury's voice hardened: "But how did it happen?"

"Some kids were trespassing on Plum Hill this morning. You know that summer house at the top? She was in there, with her neck wrung. Someone got her from behind. Used a pair of tights with a stick to hold it tight."

Vosper made a graphic movement with both his hands, as if he was uncorking an invisible bottle.

"And who was responsible?" Hanbury asked.

Vosper forgot the bottle and shrugged. "It wasn't a rapist or a robber, I can tell you that. Her handbag was lying beside the body. They found some papers in it. It seems our Alison wasn't quite who she said she was."

Hanbury raised his eyebrows and waited.

"Looks like there's a French connection, you might say." Vosper's eyes briefly disappeared as his face crumpled in a laugh. "Trust our Ally to have something up her sleeve. Her old man is a French crook. He's inside now, and there's a rumour that she's the one who put him there. So Ally wasn't very popular with her in-laws."

"So the police believe she died in some sort of—ah— gangland vendetta?"

112

"Maybe." With sudden violence, Vosper tugged at his bow tie and tore it off. "Or maybe not. Ally was never one to stint herself. A lot of people in Rosington didn't like her. Could be that one of them didn't want her to come back."

Hanbury said very little on the drive back to Charleston Parva. It was cooler now, and Dougal thought longingly of a hot bath. Railways might be much cleaner than in the days of steam; but they still left you feeling slightly soiled.

When they reached the Dower House, they let the dogs out for a last run in the garden. Dougal checked the water and found it was stone cold; Hanbury had let the Aga go out during the day. He returned to the sitting room to find Hanbury pouring them both a nightcap.

"Do you think Vosper was telling the truth?" he asked, out of the blue, as he passed a glass to Dougal.

"How should I know?" Dougal sounded pettish to himself: the absence of hot water rankled.

"He was born in a two-up, two-down in Bridge Street," Hanbury said. "Made his first million in the building trade. I suppose he's the Ezekiel Carrot *de nos jours*."

"What sort of a hold have you got on him?" Dougal asked bluntly. "That might have some bearing on his truthfulness."

"Oh, he has minority tastes. You know the sort of thing. He was combining business with pleasure in Cairo and someone tried to take advantage of him. I pulled a few strings." Hanbury nodded, as if applauding his own wisdom. "A longterm investment. I kept the photographs. I'm sure he's being truthful—well, as nearly sure as one can ever be. But it might not be the whole truth. He's a good poker player."

Dougal collapsed into an armchair. Hanbury let in the

dogs. David and Benji adopted a statuesque pose by the fireplace. Sophie, apparently under the illusion she was still a puppy, tried to get on to Dougal's lap; in the end it proved the lesser of the two evils to allow her to succeed.

Hanbury sat down. "If I gave you an annuity for the rest of her natural life, would you take that animal off my hands? . . . No? Oh well."

"Where's Plum Hill?"

"Ah. I was wondering if you would ask that." Hanbury pulled out a cigarette and frowned at it. "It's that hillock covered with trees in Canons' Meadow. I believe it had a castle on it at one time."

"Motte-and-bailey," Dougal said automatically. "You can see the outline of the bailey's earthworks in the meadow. Is it someone's orchard now?"

"It used to be. It belongs to the Dean and Chapter still. Technically it's supposed to be a bird sanctuary. There's a fence around it. The only legitimate access to it is from the garden of one of the houses in the Close. But there are several gaps in the fence. In my day, it used to be a popular place for—ah—assignations."

Dougal closed his eyes and tried to visualize it. The thickly wooded mound was to the east of what had once been the tithe barn of the medieval abbey. Indeed, the barn was so close to the mound that they seemed almost organically connected. Beneath the trees was a tangled mass of undergrowth. He couldn't recall a summer house.

"There's a clearing at the top of the hill," Hanbury said. "The summer house is in the middle. It was pretty dilapidated thirty years ago. God knows what it's like now."

"I suppose the police will have thought out the implications." Dougal opened his eyes. Sophie stirred and

114

licked his chin. A wave of foul breath swept over him. "Vosper had."

"It doesn't require much mental sophistication. It's unlikely that any outsider would have known Plum Hill, let alone how to get into it after dark. I assume it must have taken place at night. So—either Alison escorted her killer up there, or the killer came from Rosington."

"The alternatives aren't mutually exclusive."

"Of course not." Hanbury looked away. His tanned face should have looked even more tanned in the candlelight. Somehow it seemed paler.

The police arrived unheralded as Dougal was cooking breakfast.

There were two of them from the local CID. They drove an unmarked car and, obeying some unwritten law of country living, came to the back door. Perhaps they felt they belonged with the tradesmen.

Dougal offered them tea, which they accepted, and bacon sandwiches, which they declined. The chairs creaked beneath their weight as they sat down at the kitchen table. Both of them were broad men with slow movements and wide, flat faces. They wore creased suits and unfashionably wide ties. The younger one sported a moustache.

"You don't mind if I carry on with breakfast? The bacon's nearly done."

Sergeant Lewis, the older of the two, nodded. Dougal wondered if he had imagined a touch of condescension: the police were judges of normality if anyone was, and perhaps normal people were supposed to have their breakfasts before ten o'clock in the morning.

His hands shook slightly as he turned the bacon. The presence of the police always induced in him a panic-stricken sense of guilt, however innocent he knew himself to be. Lewis and his sidekick—Detective Constable somebody—made it worse by their lack of smalltalk; maybe this was an interrogation technique. He wished that he and Hanbury had discussed how they would handle the police. It was important to have matching stories. Of course, he himself had done nothing wrong. Not this time. He wished he could be so sure about Hanbury.

He flipped the bacon on to the slices of bread. Hanbury's sandwich went into the hot cupboard. He carried his own to the table and sat down. The arrival of the police had killed his hunger; but normal people ate breakfast.

"Mr. Hanbury will be down in a moment. Do you want to talk to me as well?" He bit into the sandwich; molten butter and bacon fat ran down his chin.

The DC pulled out a notebook. Lewis asked Dougal for his name, address and occupation. He waited until Dougal had swallowed his second mouthful before continuing.

"We're looking into the death of Madame Alison Garance." Lewis anglicized the pronunciation. "She died Monday night or early Tuesday morning. We're talking to everyone who was at that party at the Vineyards on Monday. But I hear you met her before that?"

Dougal nodded. "Sunday afternoon. I'd spent most of the day in Rosington, but she was here when I got back. That must have been around four o'clock. She was staying in Cambridge—the University Arms, I think—and had dropped by for tea. She left soon after I arrived."

"She and Mr. Hanbury were old friends?" Lewis contrived to make the question sound faintly salacious.

"I believe they had known one another when they were young." Dougal took another bite; a strip of bacon detached itself from the bread and fell on to his lap. He picked it up and ate it: *Damn dignity*.

Lewis said: "Didn't it strike you as odd that Madame

Garance came here? I mean, you'd've thought she'd want to see her family first."

The bacon gave Dougal a few seconds' grace before he needed to reply. It would be safest to assume that the police knew at least as much as he about Alison's life in Rosington: it was a small town; she had belonged to a well-known family; and her face had been more memorable than most.

"Perhaps she was testing the water," he said. "She hadn't seen her family for years, had she? She might have been uncertain about the reception they'd give her."

"And what was the reception like?"

"As far as I could tell, it was fine." Dougal hesitated. "Of course, I don't know the people very well."

Lewis asked him to name the guests whom he knew and to describe any others he could remember. When he had finished, the Sergeant sat back and scratched his cropped hair.

"Peter Carrot, now," he said casually. "Was he pleased to see his mum?"

It was too casual. Lewis must have heard—from Pantry or Janet Carrot?—about their conversation in the dining room.

"He seemed a little upset," Dougal conceded. "I had a chat with him, actually." He looked across the scrubbed pine table at the two policemen, in the hope they would take eye contact as a sign of frankness. "I got the impression that he'd expected his mother to be more . . . enthusiastic about seeing him again."

"He left early?"

"That's right."

"And then you had a phone call."

Dougal had been afraid of this. "Yes. It was Sally—she lives with Peter Carrot." He could see no way to keep her out of this. "She was worried about how Peter was taking it all, so she asked me over."

"You knew her before, then?"

"I'd seen her." Dougal mopped his plate with the last crust. "And Peter had told her that he'd talked to me."

"I see." Lewis didn't bother to ask for the address of Peter and Sally. He changed tack without warning: "How long have you known Mr. Hanbury?"

There was a faint ironic stress on the "mister," and the sergeant's voice was perceptibly harsher. Even the "known" carried a suggestion of carnal knowledge in the biblical sense. With a shock of surprise, Dougal realized he was being bullied. He still cherished a naïve belief that the police didn't do that sort of thing—or at least not to people with middle-class accents and white skins. His immediate reaction was anger; but he tried to conceal it. Lewis would be expecting either anger or fear and would know how to deal with them.

"Let me see," he said mildly. "It must be two or three years now. I met him in London. He asked me to the wedding, or course. After Mrs. Hanbury died—I'm sure you know about that—I came down to keep him company for a few days."

"Nice to have friends." Lewis didn't attempt to disguise his sarcasm. "Right. What did you do on Monday evening?"

"Not much." Dougal poured himself another cup of tea; the policemen refused a refill. "I came back here after seeing Sally—must have been about eight o'clock. I made myself some supper, took the dogs for a walk and read. Mr. Hanbury came back about half-past eleven. We talked for a while, and went to bed."

The Sergeant didn't ask if they had gone to bed together; but he gave the impression he was thinking it. "No disturbances in the night?"

Dougal shook his head. He wondered if he would have

118

heard if Hanbury had gone out during the night. David and Benji, who slept in the kitchen, wouldn't have barked at him. Sophie would; but she might not have heard him—she had formed the unfortunate habit of sleeping in Dougal's room, and besides, she was rather deaf.

"And where did you go yesterday?"

So there had been watchers at the railway station.

"Cheltenham. I had to go to the library."

"Why Cheltenham?" Lewis demanded angrily. "There're libraries a lot nearer than that."

Dougal felt he had won an obscure victory. He modelled his voice on that of a particularly pompous tutor he had once had: "But not with Cheltenham's newspaper files. The provincial press is the backbone of local history."

"Ah!" said a voice from the doorway. "The constabulary at breakfast. May I join you?"

Hanbury strolled into the room with an unlit cigarette between his fingers. The door had been ajar, and Dougal wondered how long he had been standing on the other side. The bathroom overlooked the yard at the back: he might well have seen the arrival of the police. Whether by luck or by intention, his timing was perfect.

Lewis scraped back his chair and stood up. "Mr. Hanbury? I'm Detective Sergeant Lewis; this is—"

"Don't be so formal, Kevin." Hanbury beamed and held out his hand. "It *is* Kevin, isn't it?"

Lewis admitted that it was.

"I thought as much!" Hanbury seized the policeman's hand and shook it vigorously. "I remember when you were the youngest under-age drinker in the Black Pig."

Ten

The telephone rang as Dougal was washing up. Hanbury threw down the tea towel and went to answer it. Sophie, who had been snoozing on Dougal's bed, could be heard barking indignantly above their heads.

When Hanbury returned a few minutes later, he was smiling. He lit a cigarette but made no move to pick up the tea towel.

"Really rather gratifying," he said. "That was Leo Cumblesham. He wants me to pop over to school this afternoon. They're having a committee meeting of the Old Rosingtonian Society. I've been co-opted to fill Molly's place until the next election."

Dougal wrung out the dish cloth. "I thought it was a boys' school."

"It was, until about ten years ago. Then they started having girls. The girls eventually became ORs in the natural course of things. But there was no one to represent them on the committee. None of the real Old Girls had sufficient *gravitas* for the job, so they made Molly an honorary Old Girl. Leo—ah—hinted that if I wanted to stand for election in the New Year, he didn't think there would be much opposition."

Hanbury strolled up and down the kitchen while Dougal finished the drying up. His pleasure was self-evident. Some of it, no doubt, was due to Cumblesham's phone call; but he was also feeling triumphant, Dougal suspected, because of the way he had handled Lewis. The policeman had been pink about the ears when he and his colleague left. Hanbury claimed that he had sabotaged the interview by dredging up memories of the Sergeant's adolescence.

But the police and the murder of Alison Garance appeared to be a long way from Hanbury's mind at present. His attention was focused on the OR Society. He told Dougal about the bitter feud which had developed between Cumblesham and Pantry during the last year's elections. Cumblesham—himself an Old Boy as well as a former headmaster—had been president for several years. Pantry, however, was not an OR—Marlborough had had the privilege of educating him; but he believed that his unique position in the school and his length of service on the staff more than compensated for this irrelevant technicality. Pantry argued that, since committee members need not necessarily be ORs, there was no reason why the president should have to be one.

The contest had been hard-fought, with Pantry lobbying viciously for a change in the electoral qualifications. Cumblesham, with the magnanimity of victory, had bestowed an Honorary Vice Presidency on his unsuccessful rival; but this, it was generally believed, had only increased Pantry's resentment.

"Of course," Hanbury said thoughtfully, "the ORS committee may be a prelude to greater things. It's often used as a sort of training ground for the Board of Governors. Molly was a governor, you know."

"But why do you want to be on all these committees?" Dougal demanded. "It's hard work and no pay. And probably very boring."

121

Hanbury shrugged. "It's not in my nature to take a back seat. You know that. Besides, I want to put something back into the community."

Dougal looked sharply at him. It was difficult to believe that Hanbury would ever give something away unless he was reasonably sure that he would receive at least twice as much in return.

Hanbury quickly changed the subject, as if his social conscience was not something he cared to discuss. "I don't suppose you'd care to come? You could wander round the prison house during the meeting. I gather one has tea afterwards, and I'm sure you'd be welcome to join us."

"Okay." Dougal had nothing better to do, and he was curious about the school. "I could take Sophie—she needs a walk."

"I suppose so." Hanbury wrinkled his nose. He stuffed his hands in his pockets and stared out of the window; he rocked gently back and forwards on his heels. "The trouble with the Board of Governors is that Westmoreland's the chairman. It's always a member of the Cathedral Chapter. Stride's a governor, too; that man's got the cathedral influence in his pocket. Stride would oppose any move to make me a governor, and that means Westmoreland would as well."

"Is Stride on the ORS committee?"

Hanbury nodded. "He's everywhere. To give the devil his due, he's come a long way in two years. He's really been quite adroit." Hanbury chuckled. "But to my mind he's made one mistake. He's concentrated too much on the cathedral and the school; he hasn't paid enough attention to the Claud Vospers of this world."

"Well!" said Mr. Pantry. "You'll never guess what a little bird told Grandpa this morning." He settled back more comfortably in the front passenger seat of the Range Rover and waited for suggestions. He had telephoned at lunchtime to beg a lift into school for the committee meeting.

Hanbury pulled away from Pantry's house. "Something about Alison, I imagine."

Hanbury's left hand was resting on the gear stick. Pantry gave it a playful tap. "Don't rush your fences, James. That was another little bird. The first little bird wasn't such a little one, actually. It was Cynthia Stride. I really think a diet would be wise, don't you? But one can hardly take her aside and tell her. Still—"

Hanbury skilfully blocked the threatened digression. "What did Cynthia have to say?"

"I ran into her outside Sainsbury's. Or rather she ran into me. Literally. She's got one of those wretched shopping trolleys and it went right over my foot. And she didn't apologize. But she did condescend to notice me. She asked me to give Jon's compliments to the committee and say he couldn't come this afternoon. Cynthia didn't even give a reason. Well really!"

Pantry occupied the next mile with a tirade about people who nursed vipers in their bosoms and other people (presumably vipers) who bit the hands which fed them. Dougal enjoyed the lecture from the safety of the back seat, where he was out of Pantry's reach. It soon became obvious that Cynthia Stride's hauteur and her husband's casual attitude to his responsibilities were only significant to Pantry in relation to something else. This was a move to raise the society's subscription; it had been proposed by Cumblesham at the last meeting and seconded by Stride. The identity of the proposer made certain Pantry's opposition, and anyone who agreed with Cumblesham was of necessity declaring war on Pantry.

"Poor Leo." Mr. Pantry shook his head with great solemnity. "I wonder sometimes if we've taken advantage of his good nature and overladen him with responsibilities. He *is* getting on. Rather woolly-minded, I fear. Perhaps a younger man is needed? Fresh blood. A new perspective." He glanced rapidly and appraisingly at Hanbury. "Don't you agree, James?"

Dougal recognized he was listening to the opening stage of delicate and complicated negotiations. In return for Hanbury's support against Cumblesham, Pantry would mastermind a presidential campaign to put Hanbury—a former head of Mr. Pantry's house—on the summit of the Old Rosingtonian Society.

Hanbury was encouraging though non-committal. He used his favourable bargaining position to persuade Pantry to talk about his other little bird.

"Do you remember Derek, duck? Or was he a little before your time?" Pantry draped his arm over the back of the seat and managed to touch Dougal's knee. "Derek Ainslie," he explained. "Charming boy—another of my grateful patients. He's Assistant Chief Constable for the county now. I rang him up this morning. 'Derek,' I said, 'I didn't sleep a *wink* last night with this terrible business hanging over me.' "

With a little help from Hanbury, Pantry came to the point with commendable rapidity. The *Sûreté* had confirmed that Alison Garance was the wife of a man who had made a fortune from siphoning other people's centimes out of their bank accounts. Her husband, had suddenly announced that he planned to share the proceeds and the rest of his life with another woman. Alison, understandably bitter, had been indiscreet, with the result that her husband and three of his colleagues were now in prison. The colleagues—and possibly the husband—were believed to have taken out a contract to kill Madame Garance. Alison had every reason to change her name and flee to England.

The police were continuing to investigate the possibility of a local angle, but they were unofficially convinced that a contract killer from France was responsible for Alison's death. According to Janet Carrot, a man had telephoned Alison at the Vineyards on Monday evening; she described his accent as "foreign"; at the time Alison had said it was a friend ringing to make sure she had arrived safely. It seemed likely that Alison had arranged the rendezvous on Plum Hill herself, perhaps in the belief that the man was bringing her money. Most of the stolen francs had not been recovered.

"How convenient," Hanbury said drily. "If we have to have murder in Rosington, let the killer be an outsider—and a foreigner to boot."

"They even had a clue—a cigarette end, just like they have in the books. Derek was awfully pleased. It was French, you see—a Caporal."

Pantry was staring at Hanbury's profile. Suddenly he glanced back over his shoulder at Dougal, as if gauging the response to his words. The old man's face was purged of expression, like a sleeping child's.

The silence lasted no more than five seconds, but they felt like minutes. Dougal looked away from Pantry and out of the window. On one side of the road, the flat farmland had given way to a high brick wall, topped with broken glass. Hanbury slowed and turned left into a winding, tree-lined drive.

"That happens to be the brand I smoke," he said casually.

Pantry winked at Dougal. "So it is, James. So it is."

Most of the school's buildings were grouped around Big Side, the main playing field. Beyond them stretched more playing fields, tennis courts and a swimming pool. The whole site was girdled by an irregular tract of trees and

125

unkempt bushes which—according to Hanbury—was known as the Wilderness.

But some of the buildings were inconveniently remote from Big Side. Among them was the Quad, the oldest of the classroom blocks. The OR committee used the staffroom there for their meetings during the holidays.

The Quad was a long, single-storey range which straggled round three and a half sides of a square. Hanbury parked in the middle.

"This is the quad with a *small q*," Pantry explained to Dougal; he waved his hand, indicating the playground. "A *large Q* signifies the classrooms and so forth as well."

Dougal expressed his gratitude for this further insight into the semantics of Rosington School. Hanbury, guessing that Pantry was capable of expatiating indefinitely on this topic, took the old man by the arm and led him away. They showed Dougal where the staffroom was. Pantry told him to turn up for tea in about an hour's time, for meetings rarely went on for longer than that. "I'm afraid poor Leo has a very short attention-span these days."

Sophie, exhibiting the contrariness which was the foundation-stone of her personality, decided that she couldn't be bothered to go for a walk; she preferred to stay in the back of the Range Rover and catch up on her sleep.

Dougal soon realized that he would have difficulty in filling the hour. The school was an unlovely architectural mixture of Victorian redbrick and postwar glass and concrete. Though some members of staff lived on the site with their families, the place as a whole seemed uncomfortably deserted, like an earthbound *Mary Celeste* floating in the Fens.

He wandered through classrooms and corridors which smelt of chalk, polish and old food. It was the smell which made any school remind you of your own, Dougal de-

126

cided; therefore, when he visited a school, he felt like a ghost revisiting his childhood. It was difficult to understand why people like Hanbury and Stride, Cumblesham and Pantry, wanted to be ghosts in their own lives. An old school tie wasn't just an article of dress; it shackled you to your past.

The sky had been overcast since lunchtime. Now, just as Dougal had come to the conclusion that he would be happier walking in the Wilderness, it began to rain. The drops of water were large and heavy. Dougal stood at one of the corridor windows and watched as the asphalt surface of the quad was transformed from a light, matt grey to a glossy approximation of black in less than a moment. Unless he wanted to share Sophie's dormitory, he would have to stay under cover here for the time being.

He pushed open another door and found himself in the school library. It was a long, high-ceilinged room with large windows of a vaguely ecclesiastical design; Dougal labelled it in his own mind as Budget Victorian Gothic. The bookcases and other furnishings were relatively new, which suggested that the room had not been built as a library. The books were so tidy that they looked as though they were on parade.

The sight of books, despite their military appearance, cheered Dougal up. There must be something here which would keep him occupied, more or less pleasurably, until tea time. He strolled along the shelves, intending to begin by getting an idea of what was available.

In the end bay, near the encyclopaedias, a block of pink volumes caught his eye. There were about twenty of them, bound in leather. Time had mellowed some of them to a dusty rose; but the later volumes were stridently pink. Each of their spines bore the same title, picked out in silver letters: *The Rosingtonian*.

Dougal chose a volume at random. It contained the school magazines for 1930–34. A bookplate inside the front cover informed him that this book had been donated to the school library by the Old Rosingtonian Society.

He found what he wanted on the shelf below. There were two volumes for the 1950s. He took them to a table. Before sitting down he lit a cigarette; the waste-paper basket, or *fug-box*, as Pantry would call it, would make a perfectly adequate ashtray. If you were going to be a ghost, you might at least have the pleasure of breaking the rules with impunity.

Stride, Jermyn and Hanbury had all left their marks on the decade. Their names appeared first in a list of new boys. As time went by they were mentioned more frequently. At first their achievements were chiefly athletic. Stride had been, appropriately enough, the school's junior hundred-yard champion. Hanbury had captained the Colts First XI. Jermyn had clinched his house's victory in the junior inter-house rugger competition with a stylish try in the last thirty seconds of the match.

Once the trio had reached the Sixth Form, evidence of intellectual pursuits mingled with the sporting achievements. Hanbury had contributed a poem on the Officers' Training Corps to the literary section of the magazine. It began:

> We long and love to march in threes,
> It does our aesthete senses please.

In the same issue, Jermyn won adulatory reviews for his performance as Jack Worthing in *The Importance of Being Earnest* (Producer: E. St J. Pantry). Stride was made a probationary house prefect.

In the *Rosingtonian* which dealt with the events of the last Summer Term, there was no hint of the scandal which had nearly wrecked the careers of two of the three boys.

By this time, all were school prefects: Hanbury and Stride were heads of their respective houses; and all of them played for the First XI. Dougal studied the team photograph.

Hanbury, a debonair and dazzling figure in white cricketing flannels, sat in the centre of the picture, as befitted the captain. He was slimmer than he was now, and his hair was darker; but he was immediately recognizable. He and one or two others wore striped caps, which presumably indicated that they were the proud possessors of school cricket colours. It was a black-and-white photograph, but Dougal had little doubt that the stripes were pink and silver.

Jermyn and Stride were among the four people who stood in the back row. Both of them were lanky and fair-haired; they squinted into the sun behind the photographer. Hanbury had already acquired his adult form; these two were still adolescents. Stride's jowls looked heavy; perhaps they were an indication that surplus fat would creep over him in later life. Dougal made an effort and superimposed his knowledge of the man on this photograph of the boy. It was easy to see a family resemblance of sorts between Stride and Jermyn; but Dougal wondered if it would have occurred to him if he hadn't known beforehand that they were cousins.

Dougal glanced as his watch. Tea time was still twenty minutes away. The rain was tapping on the windows, like the fingers of thousands of ghosts who wanted to come in. He continued to turn the pages, despite the fact that his three subjects had left the school.

A familiar name leapt up at him from a section headed *News from Old Rosingtonians*:

Jon Stride writes that he will be sailing from Southampton on May 25 aboard the *S.S. Pacifica*. He's sad to leave all his friends in the Old Country, but duty calls—he is to take over the family business. Never mind, he says—he'll just have to start a branch of the OR Society in Sydney!

Dougal lit another cigarette. He remembered belatedly that he was trying to keep his consumption down to ten a day; and this one was number twelve.

But he needed consolation after finding that date. According to Magdalene Fleetwood, Jermyn was last seen alive (apart from by his murderer) on May 23. She found his body, nearly four weeks later, on Friday, June 18, as far as he could tell. Judging by the stage of decomposition reached by the corpse, the murder must have taken place in May.

In other words, it was physically possible that Stride had murdered Jermyn. Another name had to be added to the list of suspects. Stride might have been out of the country when Jermyn's body was found; but, contrary to Dougal's previous assumption, he might not have been when Jermyn was actually murdered.

The tinkle of distant tea cups roused Dougal from his abstraction.

He looked out of the window. A sturdy little woman, sheltered from the rain by an enormous black umbrella, was pushing a metal trolley through the puddles in the quad. The umbrella had been lashed to one of the tubular hand-rails of the trolley. On the top shelf stood a large urn of gleaming aluminium which emitted puffs of steam. The equipage had a martial air: it might have been the prototype of a steam-powered military vehicle, designed to cope with rough country.

Dougal left the library and reached the corridor in time to hold open the door which led out into the quad. A split-second later, the trolley surged into the corridor, pulling the woman in its wake. Dougal had the impression that the net result would have been precisely the same if he had not opened the door; the trolley seemed as oblivious to obstacles as Sophie was in similar situations.

The driver looked up at William. "You're not having tea with that committee, are you? They said twelve cups and saucers and no one's told me any different. And if anyone thinks I'm making another trip back to the kitchen in this weather, they can think again."

"I was hoping for some tea," Dougal admitted. "But I think Mr. Stride's away, so I could use his cup."

The woman grunted; the truculent expression stayed on her weatherbeaten face. She shoved the trolley along the corridor, turned it sharply through ninety degrees and brought it to a halt outside the door of the staff common room. The tea cups rattled against one another on the lower shelf.

The noise seemed to act as a signal. Leo Cumblesham opened the door from the inside and seized the hand-rail at the front.

The woman relinquished her hold on the trolley. "Mrs. Hind says to say there's no chocolate biscuits." She smiled malevolently. "You'll just have to make do with Rich Tea."

She unhooked the umbrella, scattering droplets of rain over the trolley, the tiled floor, Cumblesham and Dougal, and stormed away down the corridor.

"The school finds it very hard to get the right sort of domestic staff," Cumblesham said in a throaty whisper. "Too cut off, you see. James was just coming to look for you."

He pulled the trolley into the staffroom. The eleven committee members gathered round it. Their eagerness

131

was tempered by a certain apprehension.

"I don't know why it is," Pantry said querulously, "but when this trolley appears I always feel like a Trojan who's just been introduced to the wooden horse."

In the distance, the door to the quad slammed behind the Grecian tea lady.

"It's quite simple." Cumblesham half-turned to address Dougal and Hanbury; the manoeuvre put Pantry behind him and effectively cut him out of the conversation. "On one occasion they made the tea in the urn but didn't take out the coffee grounds they'd put in it last time. Stale biscuits are a favourite trick, or milk that's gone off. I'm afraid they don't like us in the kitchen."

Pantry outflanked Cumblesham by slithering between the trolley and the wall and appearing at Dougal's elbow. "I see we have a liberal sprinkling of rainwater on the biscuits today. It's really quite absurd: we're paying for this privilege. I think I shall raise the matter formally at next month's meeting."

"For God's sake, Evelyn, don't do that." Cumblesham began to pour the tea. "You know what the head said last time, when you—"

"Someone has to make a stand. It's the thin end of the wedge, don't you agree, my dear James? The next thing we know, the cooks will want to turn the school into a communist co-operative, and where shall we be then, eh? Answer me that."

"Don't be absurd." Cumblesham passed the first cup to Hanbury, who looked at it carefully and passed it to Dougal.

"No tea for me, thank you." Hanbury delved into his pocket. "Anyone mind if I smoke?"

"Of course not," said Pantry and Cumblesham simultaneously. Pantry continued: "I'm so glad we've sorted out that little business about the subscriptions. When I think of the hardship—the price of human suffering—that a twenty-five per cent rise would have caused, especially among our older members—and, as you know, many of them have little more than their pensions to rely on."

"Ignoring a problem doesn't solve it," Cumblesham snapped. "It's all there in the auditors' accounts. We'll have to reconsider next year, and the rise will be a bigger one because of the delay."

"Nonsense, Leo," said Pantry indulgently. "One day you must let me take you through the accounts. It's all a question of interpretation."

There was a lull in the conversation as Pantry bent down to pour his tea. He was still between the trolley and the wall. Other committee members had drawn closer, cutting off his exits. Cumblesham took advantage of this by edging Dougal and Hanbury over to the far side of the room.

"Poor Evelyn," he rumbled. "Not as young as he was, of course. Look here, James, we've rather flung you into the deep end with this committee. Why don't you come over and have a drink this evening? After dinner perhaps." He turned to Dougal. Pantry had extracted himself from the group round the trolley and was moving towards them; he was already within earshot. "And you too, Mr. Dougal. We'll have a cosy little chat. Just the three of us, eh?"

Eleven

A clock ticked on the mantelpiece. Sophie wheezed rhyth-
mically on the hearthrug. Beside her were a few chewed
shreds of cardboard, the only remains of a box of chocolates which Hanbury had incautiously left unguarded in
the sitting room. The Dower House was as quiet as it
could ever be.

Hanbury had taken the Airedales with him. He had
had a sudden craving for big-city fleshpots. He was going
to buy some clothes in Cambridge, have an early dinner
there, and meet Dougal at Cumblesham's at nine o'clock.
Hanbury had invited—indeed pressed—Dougal to come
as well; but Dougal had refused. Large doses of Hanbury
were even more exhausting than large doses of Sophie.

Besides, he wanted to write to Celia.

A letter, he had realized, was the obvious solution to
this little problem of communication. The only wonder
was that he hadn't thought of it before. A telephone,
supposing he could get through to Celia in the first place,
was of course an infringement of privacy. It would give
her no option but to talk to him. And you could so easily
give, or receive, the wrong impression on the phone.

But a letter allowed you to choose your words with

as much care as you wanted. It posed no threat to the person at the other end, because he or she didn't have to read it. It offered a smaller risk of misunderstanding, because it could always be mulled over and reread. If Celia didn't feel like it, she needn't answer it.

Dougal balanced the pad on the arm of his chair. He wrote the address, the date, and *Dear Celia*. It was a good start. After a moment's thought, he added the Dower House's telephone number. It was best to leave open as many options as possible. Thinking of options, he began to wonder whether he was being too finicky, unnecessarily sensitive about feelings which perhaps did not exist. He thought about the immense gulf of ignorance which lay between himself and even the people he cared most about. For all he knew, Celia really wanted him to turn up in a sports car and whisk her off without warning for a sinful fortnight in the South of France.

I'm staying near Rosington with a friend—better add to the name of the friend, so that Celia would realize she had no call to feel jealous, assuming, of course, that she might—*called James Hanbury. Have I mentioned him to you?* Of course he hadn't: mentioning Hanbury in any detail would have meant mentioning any number of disagreeable autobiographical facts; he wanted to reassure Celia, not worry her. *His wife died very recently, and I think he needed a resident nursemaid. (Don't we all?)* He became aware that he was making himself out to be a regular good Samaritan; he was tempted to let it stand, but he didn't want to lie to Celia, and she was in any case much too intelligent to swallow it as the truth and nothing but the truth. *In fact he's paying me to stay here, so I'm not being altruistic. He wanted me to do some research. He's also trying to bribe me to take an exceptionally vile fox terrier off his hands. So far I've resisted. There are limits.*

The research is rather bizarre. James's wife was

electrocuted—the wiring here is primitive. Dougal flipped over the page. This wasn't what he meant to write: but it was the only thing he seemed capable of writing about. *The coroner and the police thought it was an accident; but the local gossips were convinced that James had murdered her for her money. James, who's somehow acquired an inflated opinion of my intellectual powers, wanted an outsider's viewpoint, which is difficult to find in this vicinity. I don't think he believes she was murdered but, if she was, he'd like to know about it.*

I couldn't find anything suspicious about the death itself—which isn't surprising because I'm not a detective. But, if it was murder, two points emerged: it would have required local knowledge; and the intended victim might have been James, rather than his wife. Since an unlimited number of people could have tampered with the wiring, for reasons I won't go into, I tried to think in terms of motive.

James's wife seems to have been Mrs. Clean: everyone knew her and everyone liked her. But James—despite the fact he went to school in Rosington, back in the 1950s—is still considered as a suspicious foreigner. People have long memories round here: when he was at school, he and two friends were mixed up in a juicy little scandal involving the local femme fatale, *whose family is still well-entrenched in the Rosington Establishment. The* femme fatale *subsequently had a bastard son and claimed James was the father; James denies this. As a result of all this, James is thought to be mad, bad and dangerous to know.*

There was a certain irony here: Hanbury certainly deserved the last two adjectives.

But that doesn't seem much reason for wanting to kill him. I'd be inclined to forget the whole thing—it's not as if James needs my help in winning over the Great and Good of Rosington; he's quite capable of conducting his own hearts-and-minds offensive. The only thing which makes me wonder whether there might be more to this than meets the eye is that two other people who were involved in the femme fatale *business have died—and they were murdered. One of James's two schoolchums was strangled in a village near Cheltenham, thirty years ago —with his old school tie; at the time, a tramp was believed to be responsible, but the case was never solved. The other victim was the* femme fatale *herself: she seems to have made a career as a French gangster's moll; she came back to Rosington on Monday; and a few hours later, someone strangled her. Everyone appears to be satisfied that a contract killer, hired by her husband's colleagues, was the murderer.*

Dougal lit the fifteenth cigarette and flexed his hand; he was beginning to wish he had brought his typewriter. *Two murders,* he continued—*separated in time and place; each of them perfectly straightforward, as far as the police are concerned, though neither of them has been pinned on a particular culprit.*

It's all perfectly satisfactory, unless you try linking the two murders with a possible attempt on James's life. There's no reason why the police should do that; I only did it because I was approaching the matter from another direction—digging into James's past in Rosington. But once you make the connection, the whole thing stinks of coincidence. You need too many hypotheses to explain each of the three events separately. I doubt if manuals of detection have much time for medieval philosophy; but it wouldn't harm them to include a section on Occam's Razor. The real problem is the motive.

If this had happened in the seventeenth century a modern scholar would weigh the probabilities and come to the obvious conclusion that

The doorbell rang.

Sophie was instantly alert and on her guard. Vibrating with fury, she stood foursquare on the hearthrug and barked. Dougal grabbed her by the collar, which made the barking slightly quieter, dragged her into the hall and shut her in the cupboard under the stairs. The barking continued but it was considerably muffled.

He opened the front door. Peter Carrot was on the step, methodically picking off the leaves from the Virginia creeper. He wore oil-stained jeans and a leather jacket; he looked as if he hadn't shaved since his mother's welcome-home party.

"You're alone, aren't you? Can I come in?"

Dougal nodded and stood back. Carrot brushed past him and led the way into the sitting room. Dougal followed, noting in passing that his guest had some knowledge of the Dower House's geography. Carrot tossed his crash helmet on the sofa and sat down beside it.

"I know he's out." It was as if Carrot didn't want to say Hanbury's name. "I met Pantry in the High Street, and he told me he'd gone into Cambridge."

"That's right." Dougal shut the door, which reduced the volume of the barking still further.

Carrot lit a cigarette. "You been interviewed yet?"

"By the police? They came this morning. Look, I'm sorry about your mother."

"Well I'm not." Carrot rubbed the stubble on his chin. "I mean, let's face it, she got what was coming to her. I didn't know her, so there's no point in pretending I cared for her."

"Still, it must have been a shock." Dougal glanced at him. "When we met at the Vineyards, you said something was going to happen. An explosion."

"Oh for Christ's sake—I was just *talking*. I didn't mean anything by it. If you'd just realized that your mum was a tart with a stainless-steel heart, you'd be a bit upset, wouldn't you?"

"Of course. I just wondered if you had anything specific in mind."

Carrot shrugged. "How could I? It was just the atmosphere in that house. Or in my head—I don't know. You didn't tell Kev what I said?"

138

"You mean Lewis? No, I didn't. I had to say we'd talked—Pantry would have mentioned it. But not what about."

"That bloke's a little shit." Carrot spoke without animosity, as if Sergeant Lewis's character was a fact of life to which he had grown accustomed long ago. "He came round to me and Sally's yesterday evening. You could practically hear the handcuffs clanking in his pocket."

Dougal grinned. "I didn't take to his interview manner either."

There was a moment of friendly silence between them. Then Carrot sighed.

"Sally said I'd been with her all Monday night, and on Tuesday morning. Kev didn't believe her. He caught her out once before, you see. A mate of mine nicked a video, and the police were trying to pin it on me. She said I was with her, but they were able to prove she was lying. Not that it mattered—in the end they didn't charge me. But it does matter now."

"Because you weren't with her?"

"How do you know?" Carrot's eyes narrowed. "Who've you been talking to?"

"No one," Dougal said gently. "But it did seem a possibility after what you just said. We're talking about alibis, aren't we?"

"Maybe."

"Why did you come here?"

"It was Sally's idea." For an instant the expression on Carrot's face belonged to a sulking four-year-old, forced to comply with an adult's command. "She said you might know more than we did. It was either you or a lawyer, and I don't trust lawyers. They take your money and give you shit all in return. And all the local ones play golf with the police. That's the way things get done around here."

Dougal made the obvious assumption: "So you weren't at home on Monday night?"

"All right, so I wasn't. And I didn't kill my mother, either. You try convincing Kev of that."

"Well, where were you? The last I heard was that you went out for a drink early in the evening." Dougal lit the sixteenth cigarette. "How long did that go on for?"

"I don't know, exactly. Christ, I had a skinful. I just wanted to drink and drink until everything floated away." Carrot laughed. "After about the fourth pint, you really believe it will."

"You were with friends?"

Carrot nodded. "We went to about six pubs. Ended up in a place near the station. It's got a good landlord. After closing-time he let us go on drinking in his back room." He frowned. "I think we might have played poker. I don't know when we left—it was after midnight."

Until this point in the early hours of Tuesday morning, Carrot's story could be supported by witnesses. He had told the police that he had gone back to his flat at about eleven o'clock in the evening: to have told the truth would have involved the admission of after-hours drinking. His two companions lived near the railway station, so Carrot had set off down Bridge Street by himself.

"I meant to go home, I swear it." He shot a bewildered look at Dougal. "But when I reached the end of Bridge Street, I didn't turn right for Bishopsbridge; I went left, up the hill."

"To the Vineyards?"

Carrot waved his arm, like a blind man feeling for obstacles in his path. "I knew which room my mother would be in. I . . . I wanted to see if the light was on."

The marketplace had been deserted and the Vineyards was in darkness. In the middle of the marketplace was the fountain which the town had erected to commemorate

140

the Silver Jubilee of King George V, during the mayoralty of Ezekiel Carrot. Peter Carrot had set down on the parapet.

"I suppose I was tired—I don't know. I wasn't thinking of anything. I wanted a cigarette but I didn't have any matches."

And then he heard two sounds: a screech of metal, followed almost immediately by a click which was like the hammer of a revolver falling on an empty chamber.

"I only heard it because it was so quiet. But I knew what it was, right away. It was the garden gate at the Vineyards. First the bolt, then the latch. I used to use it at night when I lived there. It always made a noise, however much you oiled it, but it was quieter than going by the front door."

The garden gate ran into Monks Lane, an alley which went north from the marketplace to the left of the Vineyards. Carrot could hear footsteps coming down the lane. He stood up and tiptoed to the far side of the fountain. The lighting was poor in the centre of the marketplace; if he craned his head, he could see without being seen.

He recognized his mother at once, by the way she walked. He wasn't sure what she was wearing—jeans, probably, with something dark on top. She made directly for the fountain: for an instant Carrot thought she must have seen him from the house and was coming to meet him. But then she veered away, down the hill. She was walking fast; and Carrot believed she was trying to keep in the shadows.

It was easy to follow her at a safe distance. He used his ears rather than his eyes, and was guided by the tapping of her heels. His own rubber soles made no noise.

Alison turned into Bridge Street. A few seconds later, a car came by travelling in the opposite direction.

"You know what she did? As soon as she saw it coming

she nipped into this doorway. No hesitation"—Carrot snapped his thumb against his finger—"just like that. She was . . . *furtive*."

The car had apparently made her more cautious. Every now and then, she glanced back. Carrot was compelled to drop further behind; often he followed her example and took refuge in doorways. On one occasion he thought she had seen him. He pressed himself into the welcoming shadow of someone's porch and counted to a hundred; his ears strained to catch the sound of footsteps coming towards him. Finally he plucked up his courage and peered down the street.

She had vanished.

"I knew where she'd gone. She was by the gate into Canons' Meadow. It had to be there. If she'd walked on down the street, or crossed the road and gone down to the river, I'd've heard her."

"Could she have gone into one of the houses?" Dougal asked.

Carrot shook his head. "When I last saw her, she was by the gate. On either side of it is this wall. At that point, the meadow comes right down to Bridge Street. There's nowhere else she could have gone. It's grass just inside the gate, so her shoes wouldn't make any sound."

But when Carrot reached the gate, he could hear nothing. The meadow sloped up to the buildings of the close. It was unlit, of course. The single lamp which burned outside the Porta served only to emphasize the darkness.

"Christ, it was weird. I've known that place all my life. I knew Plum Hill was up there on the left, and the cathedral was on the right: but they weren't there any more. It was like I'd walked into another country. Up ahead, I thought I heard footsteps. But I wasn't sure." He shivered, as if a private fear had suddenly slipped up into his conscious mind. "It could have been *anything*."

He forced himself up the hill, walking on the grass and followed a course which ran parallel to the gravel path leading up to the Porta. At the time, he thought his mother must be visiting someone who lived in the close.

"Why did you think that?" Dougal interrupted. "She could have got into the close from the High Street, through the Sacristan's Gate."

"No, she couldn't. All the public gates are locked at midnight. The one in Canons' Meadow should be too, but it never is. The verger's too lazy to walk down there."

Carrot had gone perhaps fifty yards when he tripped over a tree stump which sent him sprawling on to the gravel path; the fall had driven the air out of him in a gasp which, he was sure, must have been audible all over the meadow. He had rolled off the path at once and pressed himself face downwards in the long grass.

"I just lay there, listening. It seemed like hours." His hand shook as he lit another cigarette. "I kept wishing to God I was in bed with Sally. And there were noises—rustlings—"

"And?" Dougal prompted.

"And nothing." Carrot shrugged. "I fell asleep."

Dougal resisted an hysterical temptation to laugh. The last thing he expected from Peter Carrot was a shaggy dog story.

"That's what happens when I'm scared. It's not my fault. Some people are like that—it's *biological*. And remember, I'd had maybe twelve or fifteen pints that night. That's quite some nightcap."

"Okay, you went to sleep. When did you wake up?"

Carrot shrugged. "It was still dark. I was cold and stiff and wet. I could hear nothing. I went home as fast as I could. It was a little after four when I got home."

"Did Sally wake up?"

"Oh, she was waiting for me—she hadn't gone to bed.

143

She made me have a bath, and then I slept until about midday."

You little sod, Dougal thought. *You don't care that she spent the evening and half the night worrying about you. It simply doesn't occur to you.*

"The question is," Carrot said, "what do we tell the police? They're itching to pin it on me, I know they are. Kev doesn't believe my alibi. I'm the perfect suspect: everyone would be glad to get rid of me, and they'd all say I'd killed my mother because she treated me like a piece of shit. And then they'd think of old Ezekiel and say, well, violence runs in the family, doesn't it."

"And did you kill her?"

There was a moment of frozen silence. Expressions flickered over Carrot's face, like a succession of slides illustrating the emotions: his features rearranged themselves in turn for shock, fear, anger and, most curiously of all, amusement. The amusement grew until he burst into laughter.

"I don't know—I really don't know. Maybe I was so pissed I didn't know what I was doing. But as far as I can remember, it happened like I said."

Dougal believed him—*as far as he could remember.* "So— you think that if you tell Lewis what really happened, you're setting yourself up for him; and if you don't, you're afraid he'll crack your alibi. Is that it?"

Carrot nodded.

"Did anyone see you between leaving the pub and getting home?"

"I don't think so. The whole town was dead." The last trace of Carrot's amusement vanished. "But if he's really serious, he'll question everyone—you know, door-to-door. *Someone* might have seen me. And if they did, that bastard will find them."

144

Dougal didn't give a damn what happened to Peter Carrot. But whatever he said would affect Carrot and, through him, Sally. And Sally deserved a break, even if Carrot didn't.

"I think you should say nothing. Stick to the story you've already told the police. If necessary you can add the bit about after-hours drinking. I expect your friends would testify you were in no fit state to murder anyone."

"But—"

"You see, I don't think there's going to be any door-to-door questioning to try to break your alibi. The odds are that Lewis was just going through the motions."

It took Carrot a good ten seconds to work out the implications of this: "You mean they already *know* who killed her?"

"Not exactly. But there's a rumour—look, can you keep this to yourself and Sally?" Dougal paused until Carrot had nodded—for what *that* was worth. "Your mother seems to have been mixed up with some French criminals. There was some sort of trouble—she came here to hide from them. And they sent a contract killer after her. The police think he found her."

Carrot needed longer to process this piece of information. But when he had done so, his reaction was unnerving: he giggled.

"So mummy finally got what she deserved." He slapped his leg. "Wait till I tell Sally!" Then gloating gave way to anxiety: "You're sure about this?"

"Of course not," Dougal snapped. "It's just a rumour. But if it's true, the police aren't going to waste time chasing you when they've got a perfectly good, made-to-measure alternative. If I were you, I'd just lie low." He looked across at Carrot who was absently scraping flecks of dried mud from the heel of one of his boots; his mouth was open. Dougal wondered yet again what on earth Sally saw in him. "I'm assuming, of course, that you've told me everything."

"Well . . . Sally said I should maybe mention the dream."

"What?"

"*I* don't remember it." Carrot cleared his throat. "You know how booze can make your memory patchy. You get these little blanks. Sally said that when I got home I went on and on about a nightmare I'd had—when I was asleep in Canons' Meadow."

You don't need me, you need a psychoanalyst. Aloud, Dougal said: "What was it about?"

"According to her, I said I was floating in space. All the stars had died, and it was cold and dark . . . and sort of *infinite*. And someone—or something—was whispering in my ear."

"What was the voice saying?"

"*Life with the bloodthirsty,* Sally said. *Life with the bloodthirsty.*"

Twelve

Life with the bloodthirsty, Dougal wrote. *Whispers are always hard to identify, and Carrot couldn't even tell what sex the speaker was. (Sally asked him that.) I think he did hear the voice—and I know whose it was. But I don't know when he heard it. It might have been there and then in Canons' Meadow; but it's equally possible that his dreaming mind just scooped it out of his memory.*

Dougal glanced at his watch: it was already seven o'clock; he was going to have to hurry if he wanted a meal before going to Cumblesham's.

Perhaps it doesn't really matter. After all, it doesn't add another name to the shortlist which Occam's Razor supplied. The frontrunner is still the same.

I wish you were here, Celia. You'd test all my nuts and bolts; you'd tell me off for trying to pretend all this was safely locked away in the seventeenth century; and you'd probably interpret the evidence in a completely different way. Of course I'd like to see you for another set of reasons as well. You know that, or at least I hope you do. Do write or ring if you want to.

At least he no longer had to wonder how to end the letter—not now. He scrawled *All my love, William*, ripped the sheets from the pad and stood up. Sophie, for whom the chocolates were no more than a distant memory, was already by the door, waggling her hindquarters in what she evidently believed was an ingratiating manner. She led the way into the kitchen and stood, panting and dribbling, by the door of the cupboard where the dog-food was kept.

Ignoring her, Dougal opened the Aga. It needed banking up: the coke was glowing sullenly. *All the better.* Dougal crumpled up the letter and tossed it in. For a few seconds it lay there, uncurling in the heat and giving off a thick, acrid smoke. Then it burst into flames which seemed magically bright. Random words stood out, just before they and the paper on which they were written were reduced to ashes. Dougal made a superstitious bargain with the gods of chance: *If I see those three words, it's going to be all right.* But the gods turned him down.

All my love.

It was probably fortunate that Mrs. Palmer burst into the kitchen while Sophie was consuming her supper; in the hierarchy of Sophie's simple pleasures, food ranked slightly higher than aggression.

"Is he in?" she said. She sidled round the kitchen table, to put a barrier between herself and Sophie.

Dougal shook his head. "He'll be out all evening." Mrs. Palmer's question was of course entirely rhetorical: she would have noticed the absence of the Range Rover as she came across the yard.

Mrs. Palmer glanced round the kitchen, as if cataloguing the evidence of neglect which had developed in her absence. She wore the same mackintosh as before; the rain dripped from it, forming a moat around her on the floor. But Dougal realized at once that she was here on an errand of a very different nature. Last time she had used the front door, and had not come into the house; an unstated protocol dictated the proper form for a public declaration of hostility. The back door, however, was for private persons and everyday business.

Dougal beheaded another radish. "Can I take a message?"

"You can tell him I'm coming back next week." Mrs. Palmer sniffed. "But he'll have to keep that dog chained up and get the wiring fixed. It's not right to ask someone to work in a deathtrap." Her tone conveyed not only that Hanbury was lucky to get her back, but also that she was overwhelmed by her own magnanimity.

Sophie gave her empty bowl a last, lingering lick and turned round in search of further pleasures. Mrs. Palmer edged towards the door.

"Just light cleaning, mark you. He can like it or lump it."

The door banged behind her. Dougal laughed. Hanbury had stood before the bar of public opinion; and public opinion had eventually decided he was innocent.

Dougal only wished he could share Mrs. Palmer's certainty.

When Dougal was young, he had been told that punctuality was the politeness of princes. Though he had no desire to emulate princely behaviour, it still made him feel uncomfortable if he was late.

Cumblesham lived in Palace Square, on the corner which was nearest to the parish church of Rosington. Parking was even more restricted here than it was in the rest of the city. Dougal had hoped to find a space in the few places along the wall of the churchyard; but they were all taken—and there was a police car parked on a double-yellow line nearby.

It took Dougal ten minutes to find somewhere else. In the end, it had to be the Bridge Street car park, a good half-mile away from Cumblesham's. He discovered the reason why Rosington was so congested with parked cars as he was walking out of the car park.

There was a poster on the notice board by the entrance, advertising a concert that evening in the cathedral. This at least meant that the cathedral would be open—and could be utilized as a short cut to Palace Square. The route would save Dougal two hundred yards, and had the additional advantage, since the rain was heavier now, of offering shelter for part of the way.

He reached the close by way of Canons' Meadow. There was no sign of police activity on or around Plum Hill; but the trees there could hide an army as easily as one corpse.

Just as he reached the door in the south-east corner of the cloisters, it was opened from within. A tide of people flowed out; the whole of the east walk of the cloisters was solid with concert-goers, shuffling inexorably towards him; more of them were pouring through the south door of the cathedral itself.

Dougal inserted himself with difficulty into the stream and swum slowly against the tide. It was already ten past nine; and at his present rate of progress it would be midnight before he reached Palace Square.

It became easier to manoeuvre once he was out of the bottleneck of the cloisters. He zig-zagged at speed through the rows of chairs and groups of people, earning a few raised eyebrows as he passed; you weren't supposed to hurry on consecrated ground. To his horror he caught sight of Evelyn Pantry advancing up the nave towards him. He made a swift U-turn—a conversation with Pantry would almost certainly take more time than all but the most roundabout of diversions—and scuttled into the south transept.

Pantry seized on the school chaplain who was standing

150

defenceless at the crossing beneath the octagon. Dougal darted from his secure backwater into the south aisle of the nave. It was here—by the door of the vestry where Hanbury, Jermyn and Stride had played strip-poker for the favours of Alison Carrot—that he ran into Canon Westmoreland.

The verb was not a mere figure of speech. As Dougal rounded the corner his eyes were on Pantry and the Chaplain. His left shoulder collided with the Canon's right; to make matters worse, he tripped over the Canon's foot, lost his balance and ricocheted into the arms of a verger.

The moment was made of the stuff of nightmares: Dougal was late for an appointment; he was behaving indecorously in church; and he had accidentally offered violence to two highly respected members of the community.

"Mr. . . . Um!"

"I'm so sorry." Dougal pulled himself away from the verger, whose mouth was still open with surprise. "I'm afraid I wasn't looking—are you both all right?"

Westmoreland prodded his well-padded shoulder. "There appears to be no damage," he admitted. "A nasty jolt, but no more than that. How about you, Burton?"

The verger shook his head. His lips were now pursed. He mimed his disapproval by making a great play of straightening the badge of office which was suspended on a chain round his neck.

"Oddly enough," the Canon continued, "we were just talking of Cromwell. Mr. Um," he informed Burton, "is an authority on the wretched man."

"Not exactly an authority . . ."

"Somewhere among us is a latter-day Cromwellian." In his excitement, Westmoreland seized Dougal's arm. "There is an iconoclast on the loose."

Dougal swiftly considered the possible responses. In

the end he compromised with "Good Lord!" The phrase lacked originality and was perhaps insufficiently forceful; but it was at least appropriate to the place.

"Jonathan! Cynthia! Have you heard about the vandal in the choir?"

The Strides were crossing the aisle from the nave to the south door. Cynthia veered towards her father at once, towing her husband behind her. Dougal wondered if he had imagined that flash of reluctance on Stride's face—a momentary hesitation before he allowed his wife to pull him over to the little group outside the vestry. And that begged the question: which of them was Stride reluctant to meet?

By now his defences were in place. Stride greeted everyone with his usual charm. Even the verger, a potential elector perhaps, came in for a smile and an enquiry about his wife's arthritis. Cynthia Stride asked Dougal if Hanbury had been at the concert. When Dougal shook his head, she turned to her husband.

"Jon, we really must ask Mr. Hanbury to dinner—someone's got to make the first move. You can't let that silly schoolboy quarrel go on for the rest of your lives. Life's too short—don't you agree, Mr. Dougal?"

Dougal nodded, noting in passing that Mrs. Stride had promoted him from the ranks of the Ums and granted him the accolade of a name. The honour was probably a by-product of Hanbury's social rehabilitation. It was interesting that two very different authorities had made this clear to him in the last few hours; in this respect at least, Mrs. Stride and Mrs. Palmer, like the Colonel's Lady and Judy O'Grady, were sisters under their skins.

"You've got a point, my love," Stride said smoothly. "We must look in the diary and give James a ring." He smiled down at his wife whose face was suddenly and briefly transfigured; the expression reminded Dougal of

Sophie's when he allowed her to climb on his lap. Stride patted Cynthia's arm and turned to his father-in-law. "But what's all this about vandals?"

"A hassock has been mutilated." Westmoreland inflated his cheeks. "A prayer book has been *desecrated*. It's one of the new ones which the Dean insisted we bought. I told him that going over to the ASB was asking for trouble. Though, to be fair, I suppose we can't blame this wanton savagery on our current flirtation with modern liturgy. Not directly, in any case."

"What have you done with the evidence?" Stride asked. "Perhaps the police should have a look at it."

"An excellent idea. We shall leave no stone unturned. I was about to send Burton to collect them from the choir. Burton—?"

The verger, however, had been cut away from their group by a party of German tourists who were convinced he was the Bishop of Rosington and was therefore responsible for the absence of public lavatories in the cathedral. Burton was fully occupied in denying the one and explaining the other.

"I'll get them," Stride said quickly.

Too quickly? Dougal wondered.

"That would be kind." Westmoreland added, in a lower voice: "I'd go myself, of course, but it might cause talk. You know what people are like." His tolerant shrug implied that the townsfolk of Rosington would be outraged by the sight of a canon carrying out the lowly duties of a porter.

"Where are they?"

"Cantoris side, middle row of the stalls. You can't miss it—it's the only red hassock there; all the others are green." Westmoreland shook his head sadly. "The Women's Institute did the covers, back in the early seventies. It was agreed beyond all possible doubt that they would be green.

But Mrs. Burnham *had* to do a red one. Poor Anne always liked to be different.''

Stride grinned. "And because *she*'d done it, you had to have it on show?"

"Well . . .'' Westmoreland examined his fingernails. "Let us say that the Chapter had no desire to offend the old lady unnecessarily. We must be gentle with the elderly''—his voice acquired a homiletic resonance—"and suffer their foibles.''

Dougal, to whom the last sentence had been addressed, nodded gravely. In this case, he suspected, the Chapter's natural benevolence had been reinforced by Mrs. Burnham's regular contributions to the cathedral maintenance fund.

"I'll come and give you a hand,'' he said to Stride.

The hassocks and the prayer books in the choir came in jumbo sizes, to match their surroundings, so the offer was not as absurd as it might have sounded. But Dougal's motives were not altruistic. Westmoreland's rating on the Ancient-Mariner scale was very nearly as high as Pantry's; and this errand would break the spell. By now, Dougal was nearly twenty minutes late for Cumblesham. And there was another reason to go with Stride: the man was on edge this evening, perhaps because of Dougal's presence.

Stride said nothing as they crossed beneath the octagon. But he paused at the brass gates to the choir.

"Did you say James was in Rosington this evening?"

No, I didn't. "I imagine he's at Mr. Cumblesham's by now. I'm meant to be meeting him there.''

Stride raised his eyebrows. "Let me guess. Leo's intending to do some whisky-flavoured canvassing for the ORS committee?"

"Something like that.''

"I bet I'm in his bad books.'' Stride pushed open one

leaf of the gates and they went into the choir. "There's only one crime worse than missing a committee meeting, and that's voting against him." He turned right and climbed up the three steps which led up to the middle row of stalls on the south. "Did you hear what they decided about the subscriptions?"

"I believe they're staying the same, for the time being. Didn't Canon Westmoreland say the hassock was on the other side?"

"Of course." Stride descended and crossed the choir. "A victory to Pantry. Ah—there's the offending hassock. I expect Leo is mustering his forces for a counter-attack. Some of these greens really are hideous."

Dougal, peering over Stride's shoulder, was forced to agree. Apart from Mrs. Burnham's red, which flaunted itself halfway down the row, the other hassocks were all green. But the WI had obviously failed to agree on the precise shade which should be used. The result was a striking example of the inharmonious permutations which could be achieved within a very small section of the spectrum.

"And I presume the desecrated prayer book belongs to the same stall." Stride flipped open the heavy volume, which was bound in turquoise plastic and bore the arms of the cathedral. "Here we are." He held open the front cover so Dougal could see what had been written on the flyleaf: ROSINGTON F.C. GOT NO BALLS. "Even a hint of *double-entendre*: I wonder if that was intentional?"

"The hassock looks okay." Dougal prodded it with his toe: it didn't budge. "It must weigh a ton."

Stride grunted with the effort of rolling it over. The hassock was two feet long, and one foot in height and depth. "It *does* weigh a ton. Solid horsehair, I should think. Look at the back."

The material had been slashed diagonally in both directions, probably with a penknife. The cuts had had a lot of force behind them: they had sliced through the red velvet and the hessian beneath. The neo-Cromwellian had tugged out a glistening tangle of black horsehair. Dougal thought of swastikas and sprayguns.

"So pointless, isn't it?" Stride said. "That's what offends me. If it served some purpose, you could at least understand it."

In the end they found it easiest to carry the hassock between them, with the prayer book resting on the top. They drew some curious glances as they processed back to the vestry. There were beads of sweat on Stride's face; what you could see of his complexion above the beard was flushed; his breathing was fast.

Westmoreland and Cynthia Stride had been drawn into the group of tourists, which had now been augmented by a party of Japanese and two highly articulate American students. The door to the vestry was open, though two long curtains sheltered its mysteries from the eyes of the profane.

The room smelt of old clothes and stale incense. Stride and Dougal left the hassock on the table in the middle. *It must be the same table*, Dougal thought. He tried to imagine the four of them sitting round it, watching the fall of the cards and passing the brandy bottle between them.

Typical teenage melodrama . . .

He glanced at Stride, who was meticulously removing fragments of horsehair and fluff from the jacket of his dark suit. Did he remember it? Did he ever think of Alison as she was then: infinitely desirable, a heady compound of glamour and sin? His anger must have become unbearable as the luck of the cards, and Hanbury's sleight of hand, put him out of the running.

He must have been angry to have acted as he did.

156

And later, the table would have been used for another purpose. But Stride, of course, would not have been there. It looked damned uncomfortable. Perhaps they had decided to use the carpet in the end. Only Hanbury now knew the answer to that.

But Hanbury was not a reliable source: he lacked a proper, scholarly, regard for truth.

Stride cleared his throat. "I must go and rescue Cynthia from the United Nations."

"Sorry—I was wool-gathering." Dougal added, almost without thinking: "It's like the wings of a stage, isn't it? I've never been in a cathedral vestry before."

"Oddly enough, nor have I."

He led the way out of the vestry. Dougal asked him to say goodbye to the others on his behalf.

The nave was nearly empty of people by now. Dougal walked quickly down the centre, between the rows of chairs, without looking back. He had an uncomfortable feeling that Stride was still standing by the vestry door, watching him.

The first thing he noticed as he emerged from the west door was that the night air was full of revving engines. Somewhere above his head, the cathedral clock struck the half hour.

It was still raining, and the traffic in Minster Street was throwing sheets of spray on to the pavements. To the left, towards the Porta, the road was flooded from one side to the other; a gulley must be blocked. Dougal sprinted across the street, swearing as water splashed up his trouser legs.

Palace Square was an ill-lit and irregular quadrilateral of scrubby grass and, after all this rain, mud. In front of Dougal was the parish church, eternally doomed to second-class status by the cathedral which towered over it; and beside the church was a huddle of cottages, one of which belonged to Leo Cumblesham. The square was closed to traffic, but a gravelled roadway ran down each side. Dougal chose the one on the right, which had the advantage of the shelter offered by a row of chestnut trees.

He was passing the second tree when he heard the voice. It seemed to come from the branches above his head.

"I am become like a pelican in the wilderness," it said with an odd note of pride. "And like an owl that is in the desert."

Thirteen

"Mrs. Westmoreland?"

"Psalm one hundred and two." A shadow detached itself from the bole of the chestnut and moved noiselessly towards Dougal. "It goes on: 'I have watched, and am even as it were a sparrow: that sitteth alone upon the housetop.' "

By the dim light of the streetlamps in Minster Street, Julia Westmoreland at first appeared to be in fancy dress of an ecclesiastical nature. As she drew nearer, Dougal realized that she was wearing a dark overcoat which was several sizes too large for her; the hem trailed on the ground behind her. The collar was turned up; and her hair was covered by a dark scarf.

Without warning, she switched on a torch. The beam stabbed at Dougal's face, forcing him to close his eyes. The beam moved away, panning to either side of him.

"Good," Mrs. Westmoreland said. "You're alone, Mr. Dougal." She made it sound like a virtue. "You'd be surprised how many people use Palace Square for acts of darkness."

"And Canons' Meadow, perhaps?"

159

The beam wavered, casting a loop of light across the grass. "How do you know that?"

Dougal shrugged. "It's even more private than here, after nightfall." He tried to forget how time was slipping by. A few minutes wouldn't hurt, one way or the other. "You shine a light on them?"

" 'Thy word is a lantern unto my feet' . . . psalm one hundred and nineteen . . . 'and I shine it upon them, to illuminate them in their sin.' " She added, more quietly: "Usually the man blasphemes, the girl bursts into tears, and they both run away."

"Do you look for them on most nights?"

"Not so much in the colder weather. But in the summer I sometimes go out twice. It's the tourists, you see." She edged closer to him; he could smell her warm, sour breath. "They even do it in broad daylight."

Dougal took half a pace backwards. "Have you found anyone recently?"

Julia Westmoreland shook her head. At the same time, she shone the torch, from below, on her face. It created the impression that a disembodied head was waggling five feet above the ground. The hollows and crannies of her face became bottomless shadows. The effect was eerie but also absurd, like a grown-up's conscientious attempt to frighten the children at a Hallowe'en party.

"Not since Monday night," she said. "She started it, you know—she and Frank. But the woman is always the temptress."

Frank? Frank Westmoreland, of course—the Canon's son and Julia's husband. And she—

"Now she's dead, perhaps it will stop; perhaps the Lord has answered my prayer." Mrs. Westmoreland's voice lost its conversational tone and became a chant: " 'O shut not up my soul with the sinners—' "

" 'Nor my life with the bloodthirsty.' " Dougal had

160

skimmed through the Book of Common Prayer as he ate supper. "Psalm twenty-six."

He should have felt elated that his search had paid off; instead he remembered that Cromwell's psalm-singing cavalry had been recruited from the eastern counties; and he wondered if a seventeenth-century Carrot had ridden off with a bible in his saddle-bag to fight the King.

The torch swung back to Dougal's face; he forced himself not to flinch. Her breathing in the darkness was rapid and shallow. He decided to press home his advantage; she was not used to people who fought with her own weapons.

"You followed your sister on Monday night?"

"No, I did *not*. I woke up and found she had gone. I—"

"You went down to check if she was in her bed?"

"I know—knew—Alison. She had to be *rutting* somewhere. That man had telephoned her, the one Janet later said had a French accent—"

"Later?"

"Well, all Janet said to me on Monday night was that a man had rung up for Alison. Then that horrible policeman told her about the French crooks, and she suddenly decided that the man must have had a French accent."

"Why would she do that?"

"Janet?" Julia Westmoreland chuckled unexpectedly. "Because she was scared that someone would tell the police about the row she had with Alison. After the party on Monday, Alison asked Janet for money. A loan, she called it. And Janet was *furious*. Actually, it wasn't just the money: I think Janet was upset because Alison ignored Peter. She hates it when people don't fall in with her plans for them."

"What did you do when you found Alison wasn't in her room? What time was this?"

161

"Two o'clock? Three o'clock? I don't know."

The torch made a figure of eight on the grass between them. Dougal sensed that he had lost whatever advantage he had gained from his unexpected knowledge of psalm twenty-six. Julia Westmoreland was no longer off-balance; she wouldn't respond to verbal bullying any more. But she was still malicious.

"I expect your sister—Miss Carrot, I mean—was even more furious when she heard that Alison was gone."

"If Janet knew that Alison had gone out on Monday night, it wasn't because *I* told her. Which isn't to say that she didn't know. Janet always locks her bedroom door at night—she's terrified of burglars, always has been. I knocked on the door, of course, but there was no answer." Julia sniffed. "In the morning, she said that Alison had upset her so much that she had to take *four* sleeping tablets. She takes a lot of pills, you know; if the truth were told, she can't do without them. So she *might* have been asleep."

"Or she might not have been there?"

Dougal realized at once that he had gone too far; Mrs. Westmoreland liked to draw her own innuendoes. The torch flicked across his face once more; this time it was like a whip.

"I fail to see what business it is of yours, Mr. Dougal." The puritan Carrot had been replaced with a more up-to-date version—the Carrot with an assured position within provincial society. Mrs. Westmoreland switched her line of attack: "I might just as well ask you what you're doing now—*lurking* in Palace Square."

"Just passing through on my way to the Cumble-shams.' I had to park all the way down in Bridge Street. I couldn't find anywhere nearer because of the concert."

The puritan came to the fore again: she clicked her tongue. "I've never approved of allowing God's house

162

to be used as the Albert Hall. I've made my views *quite* clear to my father-in-law. Tonight's programme of music was entirely secular." There was another click of the tongue as she changed personas again. "And I fail to see why you had to park in Bridge Street. People visiting the Cumbleshams always leave their cars in the car park of the Three Crowns. Leo has an arrangement with the landlord. *Everyone* knows that."

"I expect Mr. Cumblesham thought I'd be coming with James." Dougal shuffled a few inches closer to Cumblesham's cottage; the cathedral clock would soon be striking the third quarter. "And James must have forgotten to tell me."

Julia Westmoreland slid away on another tack. "How did you know about Canons' Meadow? Were you there?"

"Not on Monday night." Dougal paused. "But somebody else was. And they heard you."

This sudden frontal attack was a desperate gamble. It was desperate because he didn't think she would admit to having been there, and because time was running out.

The cathedral clock began to strike the third quarter.

Mrs. Westmoreland threw back her head and howled. Her sorrow was as naked as a child's.

"She was alone when I found her."

Alison? She spoke so quietly that Dougal could hardly make out her words.

"And I had *prayed*. That's why it was such a shock. Deliver my soul from the sword: my darling from the power of the dog."

According to Hanbury, Mrs. Cumblesham was popularly believed to be Rosington's most browbeaten spouse. In the privacy of the home, Cumblesham lost his benign public persona. Expert observers, such as Evelyn Pantry, argued that his wife must be a masochist; it was pointed

163

out that her closest female friend was Janet Carrot who, like her husband, treated her as an educationally subnormal maid-of-all-work. Despite Hanbury's briefing, the reality of Cumblesham's ménage came as a shock to Dougal.

When Elizabeth Cumblesham opened the door, Dougal realized that he had seen her before, though they had not been introduced. She had made a rare social appearance at Hanbury's wedding, partly because her husband was giving away the bride, and partly because Janet Carrot required her to fulfil the role of lady-in-waiting. It was she, Dougal remembered, who had prophesied that Hanbury's marriage wouldn't last.

Mrs. Cumblesham shook hands listlessly with Dougal. She was a sallow, bony woman, with the sort of complexion which always looked dirty.

"Leo is in the sitting room," she said. Lowering her voice, she added: "James hasn't turned up yet, and he's *furious*."

Dougal smiled at her; but his attempt at reassurance was foiled by a bellow which was only slightly muffled by the closed door of the sitting room.

"Elizabeth! They haven't come to talk to you on the bloody doorstep!"

Mrs. Cumblesham winced. "Oh dear. You'd better go in."

As he opened the door, a cloud of wood smoke rolled out to meet him. A small log fire smouldered in a grate which had been designed for coal. It was a chilly night for July, and the cottage had the musty smell of damp. A fire was a good idea in principle; but in practice it produced more smoke than heat.

"I'm sorry I'm late—" A fit of coughing prevented Dougal from continuing.

Cumblesham ignored the apology. "Where's James?"

He was sitting in an over-stuffed armchair, covered with black imitation leather, and clearly had no intention of standing up to greet his guest.

Dougal moved cautiously through the fog towards his host. The room was small and low-ceilinged; the furniture—another armchair and a sofa which both matched Cumblesham's, plus a large quantity of strategically placed occasional tables—combined with the poor visibility to make it a hazardous journey. He reached the one relatively clear space—the rug in front of the fire.

"Well?" snapped Cumblesham. His face was more flushed than usual. In his hand was an empty balloon glass; and on the table beside him was a half-full bottle of brandy whose label displayed the Emperor Napoleon in a convivial mood.

"I'm surprised James isn't here already." Dougal looked with astonishment at the enormous oar which was suspended above the mantelpiece. "He had to go into Cambridge this evening. I arranged to meet him here at nine. But the parking—"

"You'd better have a drink, I suppose."

Dougal interpreted this as an invitation to sit down. He chose the sofa because it was further from the fire—and from Cumblesham—than the vacant armchair. Cumblesham rummaged in a cupboard beside his chair and produced a fresh glass. He splashed brandy into it and refilled his own.

"Cheers," he said gloomily.

They drank in silence for a few seconds. Then Cumblesham gave a gusty sigh and leant forward to throw another log on the fire. Smoke billowed into the room with renewed force.

"It's been a bloody awful day, don't you think? Best thing to do is to drown it."

Dougal nodded and tried to look intelligent.

"And it's bloody awful brandy, as well. It's all I can afford on my pension. *I* haven't got an inherited income, like some people I could mention." He scowled at Dougal, who was wise enough not to take it personally. "I bet Evelyn Pantry's never even heard of *Spécialité de L'Empereur.*"

Dougal took another sip. Cumblesham launched into a long story about Pantry's pretensions to being a connoisseur of brandy. Dougal glanced surreptitiously round the room. There were trophies on the tables and team photographs on the walls; the room held no trace of Elizabeth Cumblesham and the relative poverty of his host's surroundings was as much of a surprise to Dougal as Cumblesham's bitterness had been. It contrasted sharply with the quiet affluence which characterized the houses of Cumblesham's peers in Rosington.

Cumblesham abruptly finished his story. "Where *is* James?"

"I expect he'll be here soon." Dougal could hear the cathedral clock striking ten. He debated whether decency required that he should stay for another half-hour, or whether fifteen minutes would be sufficient. "I suppose we could try ringing the Dower House."

Cumblesham shook his head. "Elizabeth did that just before you came. I told her to keep trying."

Three possibilities flitted through Dougal's mind: the Range Rover had broken down; Hanbury had found something more interesting to do; or someone had prevented Hanbury from coming. The first wasn't worth worrying about; the second was unlikely, because Cumblesham's support might be important for Hanbury's Rosington ambitions; but the third—

If Occam's Razor had been sharp enough to amputate the non-essentials and dissect accurately what remained,

166

then Hanbury's absence might be not only Dougal's fault but also permanent.

"I lay this at Jon Stride's door," Cumblesham said abruptly.

Dougal glanced in astonishment at his host. *"What?"*

"The freeze on subscriptions, of course." Cumblesham scowled. "When I think what I've done for that boy, I could strangle him. He *promised* me he would be at the meeting today. I wouldn't have tried to put through the raise if I hadn't been sure I could rely on his support. We've got two Conservative councillors on the committee, and they always follow his lead. And today they went and voted for Pantry."

He relapsed into silence, apart from little snorts of indignation which escaped him every few seconds, like steam from a kettle on the verge of boiling.

Dougal stirred in his chair. The word *boy* was worth following up. "I think James said that Stride was in your house. I presume that was before you became headmaster?"

"Both of them were." Cumblesham looked slightly less depressed, as if the memory of past triumphs had boosted his morale. "Jon Stride and Charles Jermyn: the orphan cousins. I made him my head of house. That was a mistake."

"Why was that?"

"Too bloody weak. Liked the privileges but couldn't handle the responsibilities. If I'd had any sense, I would have chosen Jermyn, poor sod. Young Charles never had much luck."

Dougal grinned. "I heard about you catching him and James with Alison Carrot after a night on the town."

"He certainly paid in full for that little jaunt. That should have warned me about the tricky ways of Master

167

Stride, if nothing else did." Cumblesham stared blearily at Dougal, and added with a certain melancholy pride: "I bet James didn't tell you about *that* episode. The sequel, as it were. He couldn't have done: I'm the only person who knows about it now—except for Stride, of course."

"I thought James and Jermyn were punished . . . well, discreetly. That nobody wanted a scandal."

"So they were. What was the point of expelling two boys near the end of their last term, just for some youthful prank? Oh, they got beaten and gated, but that was that. Pantry and I even kept it from the head. In those days, getting expelled could mark a chap for life."

And the influential Carrot family wanted the whole thing decently buried as well. No doubt some tactful little gesture was made at the time, to seal the bargain—a donation to the school, perhaps.

"But Stride talked?"

Cumblesham shrugged. "Not right away. Master Jon had an eye for the main chance. He waited till he'd left. He wanted to get into the RAF as a pilot, and he needed a decent reference from me. Not that it did him much good: they turned him down for medical reasons, apparently. Eyesight I think. So he bided his time for a month or two. It wasn't until the beginning of the next term the boys' guardian wrote to me."

"The uncle in Australia?"

"You seem to know an awful lot about it." Cumblesham's voice hardened.

"Not really." Dougal tried to dispel the cloud of suspicion which was gathering on his host's face. "I think James said something about him. You know what he's like when he starts talking about his schooldays."

This appeared to satisfy Cumblesham, who perhaps took it to mean that Hanbury found his schooldays an

168

endless source of fascination. He grunted and poured them both another drink.

"Extraordinary fellow," he said at last. "The uncle, I mean. Very Victorian in his standards. Self-made man, I believe. Between you and me, he was a bit of a cold fish. Jermyn's parents were killed in the war, and he went to live with the Strides. The mothers were sisters, or perhaps cousins—I can't remember. Then Stride's parents died in a car crash, just after the boys came to Rosington—to the Choir School that is. Boys must have been seven or eight at the time. And the uncle became the guardian. Angus somebody—Wharton, was it?"

He fell silent, staring at the fire and pursuing some half-forgotten scent in his memory. The brisk manner which usually camouflaged him had dropped away, revealing an old, tired man beneath.

After a decent interval, Dougal gently brought him back to the subject. "There were no other relatives?"

"Eh? Oh yes—there was an aunt somewhere. Wimbledon, I think. She used to have the boys in the holidays. But she died before they left the Choir School. In any case, Wharton was the legal guardian." Cumblesham sighed. "Extraordinary fellow."

"In what way?" The repetition of *extraordinary fellow* brought to Dougal's mind the nightmarish possibility that this conversation might continue to go round in circles for ever.

"I'd call him . . . Victorian." Cumblesham paused, as if he had just produced a daring new insight and wanted to admire it for a few seconds. "He wrote me a letter when the boys entered my house. Very keen on them getting a Christian education and a good moral tone: you know the sort of stuff. But he didn't want to be bothered with the boys himself. I had to find them places to stay

169

in the holidays, and so on. Caused no end of trouble. But he paid all the bills without question—and on the nail. Not like some of our parents. *Elizabeth!*"

The shout erupted from Cumblesham without warning. Dougal jerked in surprise, spilling a few drops of brandy on to his trousers. They sat in an awkward silence for thirty seconds until Mrs. Cumblesham poked her head round the door.

"Yes, dear?"

"Where's James? Have you got through to him?"

"I'm sorry, dear, but there's still no answer. I'll keep trying, shall I?"

Cumblesham nodded curtly and stared fixedly and fiercely at his wife until she gathered that she was dismissed. The pity which Dougal felt for his host was replaced by anger. The anger was not only on behalf of Mrs. Cumblesham but on behalf of himself: why did Cumblesham have to confuse everything by eliciting contradictory responses from him? The door closed with the softest of clicks.

"Bloody rude, that's what I call it." Cumblesham glanced at Dougal and frowned. "You'd think he'd have the common courtesy to let us know he was going to be late."

"Perhaps his car broke down," Dougal said, "and there wasn't a phone around." Anger made him abandon tact. "You were talking about Mr. Wharton paying the bills on time."

"And that's about all he was good for." Cumblesham glared at Dougal, as if suspecting him of being a secret supporter of Wharton. "He could afford it—owned a factory or two; made radio components, I think. Even the war must have been good for business. He was cold as charity—believe you me."

"I see." Dougal made an effort to nudge the conversation in the direction he wanted it to take: "Stride told his guardian about Jermyn being caught with Alison Carrot and a couple of empty brandy bottles?"

"Someone did. Who else could it have been?" Cumblesham paused; for an instant, Dougal wondered whether the vestiges of professional reticence had triumphed in the last moment over the alcohol-fuelled urge to confide; fortunately bitterness came to the aid of the brandy. "Wharton wrote me an extraordinary letter—sanctimonious, that's the word. He implied I'd committed a grave dereliction of duty and I should thank my stars he wasn't going to inform the governors. Said he'd been informed that Jermyn had been indulging in alcohol and fornication—those were his exact words—and would I kindly confirm this. And he hinted pretty strongly that he intended to alter the dispositions of his will."

"What did you do?"

Cumblesham made a sound which in a bear would have been a growl. "What could I do? I could hardly deny it. I wrote back, as tactfully as I could; I tried to tone down the fornication element. The old man died a few months later, and Stride scooped the jackpot."

"Neat and nasty," Dougal said. His mind was elsewhere.

"But you see what must have happened?" Cumblesham smacked the palm of his hand against the arm of his chair. "Stride tells Wharton, simply out of *greed*. He was relying on his guardian's rigid standards. And it worked; Jermyn was disinherited, and Stride got his cousin's share added on to his. Totally cold-blooded, just like his desertion this afternoon. I should've expected something like this. The boy is father to the man, and don't ever let anyone tell you differently."

In other words, Stride had no financial motive—no motive at all—for killing Jermyn. The uncle had died before Jermyn was killed, and Stride had already gained all there was to gain.

171

"Poor old Charles." Cumblesham yawned. "Then he went and got himself killed. Some people have all the luck, don't they?"

Dougal's reasoning lost its foundation at a stroke. He felt as though his mind had been buried in the rubble. Occam's Razor *should* have worked. The maxim stated that assumptions should not be needlessly multiplied. Applied to an investigation of this nature, it could be interpreted as saying that one should prefer the explanation which involved the fewest hypotheses.

"Stride's gone over to Pantry, you know," Cumblesham said owlishly. "If that wasn't the case, he would have sent in his vote by proxy. He *knew* subscriptions were on the agenda."

Postulating a single murderer for all three murders had seemed, in the circumstances, a perfectly reasonable assumption: *Entia non sunt multiplicanda*. It followed that the murderer could not be younger than his or her late forties. Here the reasoning became speculative: two of the victims—perhaps three—were connected with the vestry scandal: possibly the murderer was as well. If this was so, there were six candidates for the shortlist: Pantry, Cumblesham, Julia Westmoreland, Janet Carrot, Stride and Hanbury. He had ruled out Pantry and Cumblesham: their age made it unlikely that either of them would have been capable of killing Alison; and neither had a motive. Julia or Janet might have killed Jermyn because of what he had done to their sister; the ungovernable violence which ran in the family gave this idea a tincture of credibility. But strangling, the *modus operandi* of two of the murders, was rarely a woman's way of killing; and it was difficult to imagine either of them being able to strangle a large and vigorous youth like Jermyn.

Hanbury and Stride, however, were both physically capable of the job; and both of them could have been in

Pormon at the time of Jermyn's death. Hanbury had certainly shown himself to be morally unsqueamish on other occasions. But sexual jealousy was not the most plausible of motives for him; and why should he subsequently kill Molly?

"It's the implications that worry me," Cumblesham said suddenly. "Suppose Pantry and Stride combine. Suppose they suck James into their orbit. What then?"

Until this evening, Stride had seemed the obvious choice, on the assumption that he stood to gain financially from his cousin's death. The subsequent murders could flow from the first; the deaths of Hanbury (or even Molly?) and Alison might have been necessary, for some unknown reason, to cover up Jermyn's.

Until this evening.

Cumblesham leant forward. "Pantry's got his eye on a governorship—you mark my words. He could do *incalculable* harm."

Dougal nodded absently.

Stride and Hanbury were still at the head of the shortlist. Among the legions of intangible conjecture was one reassuringly hard fact: a male voice had telephoned Alison on Monday evening—a male whom she knew well enough to agree to meet.

But without a motive . . .

"Which is why, of course, it's so essential that James and I put our heads together. More brandy?"

Dougal shook his head. Despite himself, he grinned: it had suddenly occurred to him that as he hovered helplessly between Stride and Hanbury he was behaving remarkably like Buridan's Ass, a monster conjured up by the psychological determinism of one of Occam's disciples.

Buridan, enquiring into the nature of volition, had reached the conclusion that the will yielded always to the strongest attraction of the moment. The problem here,

Dougal remembered, was that if an ass was placed between two equal and equidistant bundles of hay, the unfortunate animal would eventually die of starvation.

"Why don't you share the joke?" Cumblesham demanded suspiciously.

At that moment, the telephone began to ring.

Cumblesham stood up and blundered towards the door; one of the occasional tables toppled on to the carpet as he passed. Dougal followed him. The bell filled his head like an alarm.

As Cumblesham opened the door, his wife reached the phone. Dougal peering over his host's shoulder, could see Mrs. Cumblesham clutching the handset as if it was a lifeline. A voice crackled inaudibly on the other end. Elizabeth Cumblesham chirped "Oh . . . oh . . . oh" in reply.

Her husband strode into the hall and seized the phone from her. "Cumblesham speaking. What's all this? . . . James? What do you mean, an *accident*?"

Fourteen

"But the doctor said—"

"What the doctor says and what I do aren't necessarily the same." Hanbury swayed slightly; his grip tightened on Dougal's arm. "I've discharged myself. I take full responsibility."

The nurse, whose dark-blue uniform gave her a paramilitary air, refused to be cowed. She merely changed her approach. "We like to keep cases like yours under observation, at least overnight. Why, only the other day, we had a man with concussion who—"

"Oh do be quiet." Hanbury waved his free hand in a gesture of irritation. With the bandage on his head, he looked distinctly oriental, like the sultan dismissing a refractory odalisque. "You've not stopped talking since we left the ward. What I need is peace and quiet, and I certainly won't get that here, with your chattering away and all those old men snoring. Come on, William."

Dougal pulled open the door which led from the hospital foyer to the car park. Hanbury edged through and ostentatiously sucked in a lungful of the damp, night air.

"Ah! Fresh air at last."

The nurse, sensing that Dougal might be the weak

175

underbelly of this particular axis, asked him if he had any medical training.

"Of course he hasn't," Hanbury snapped. "And he also lacks the lickspittle respect for authority which characterizes your profession. And he's not a bully in blue, either. Good night to you."

They walked slowly across to the Morris Traveller. Behind them, the glass door swung back with a rush of air, cutting off the nurse's parting shot in mid-flight.

Hanbury chuckled. "Childish, wasn't it? But I can't stand people with a little authority who treat everyone else as if they're five years old. It's an occupational hazard for nurses, policemen and civil servants. That woman was really most offensive when I lit a cigarette."

Dougal opened the passenger door and Hanbury slowly climbed in. As Dougal walked round to the driver's side, he wondered how much of Hanbury's anger was really due to fear. He got in, inserted the key in the ignition, but did not turn it.

"What happened, James?"

Hanbury shrugged. "I'm not entirely sure. I got to Rosington a little after nine o'clock and parked in the Three Crowns. There's a footpath from there to Palace Square—runs between the churchyard and the wall of the Bishop's garden. No lighting, but it's only about thirty yards long. I was about halfway down when something hit me. There."

He touched the bandage, just above and behind his left ear.

"I went out like a light. Whatever hit me broke the skin. I presume that whoever did it was lying in wait behind the churchyard wall. It's about the right height."

Dougal pushed aside the thought that the blow could have been self-inflicted. "Was anything stolen?"

"There wasn't time." Hanbury lit a cigarette. "By the grace of God an off-duty policeman was coming out of the Three Crowns. Apparently I gave a shout as I fell. He came to investigate. They've had the occasional mugging on that footpath before. He got me an ambulance. But there was no sign of the—ah—mugger."

"That's the official story, is it?" Dougal started the engine. "A mugger?"

"There are other possibilities, of course. But I doubt if they'd cut much ice with the police."

They drove most of the way to Charleston Parva in silence. Dougal needed to concentrate on his driving; Hanbury was perhaps more affected by the blow he had received than he cared to admit.

Half a mile outside the village, Dougal said abruptly: "Why didn't you tell me you were in England when Jermyn died? I saw your father when I went to Cheltenham. I—I gathered he was expecting a visit from you, but you never turned up. Something about running into an old school friend while you were in town."

The memory of those letters, still in his flat in Kilburn, festered in his mind.

"Dear me," said Hanbury. "You have been busy. How was the old fellow?"

Dougal shrugged in the darkness. He was at least grateful that Hanbury hadn't questioned his methods.

"Let me see . . . Yes, I did come back from Germany at some point. For a course, if I remember rightly. I don't remember any school friend. Probably a euphemism for —ah—a young lady. And at the same time as poor Charles . . . ?"

"As far as I can tell. No one knows precisely when he was killed."

"Except the murderer, naturally," Hanbury said with

177

a touch of reproof in his voice. "Well, well. It had slipped my mind entirely. It's irrelevant, in any case. Why on earth should I kill Charles Jermyn?"

The question was impossible to answer. Fortunately they turned into the courtyard of the Dower House at this point, and Dougal was saved the necessity of trying. Sophie was barking hysterically on the far side of the back door.

"Oh my God," said Hanbury suddenly. "I've forgotten the Airedales. They're still in the Range Rover at the Three Crowns. I don't suppose you could possibly nip back to Rosington and pick them up?"

Forty-five minutes later, Dougal drove the Range Rover up the hill and into Charleston Parva. He was mildly proud that he had been able to drive this tank-like vehicle all the way from Rosington without damaging anyone or anything in the process. Hanbury had insisted that, if either of the cars had to be left overnight at the Three Crowns, it would have to be the Morris Traveller.

He pulled into the yard behind the Dower House and switched off the engine. David and Benji woke up and, realizing that they were home, began to prod the back of the Range Rover with their noses and paws. For a moment, Dougal ignored their impatience.

There was a green Ford Cortina parked in the yard.

The car was unfamiliar to him. The model was several years old. The Range Rover's headlights shone full on the rear window, picking out a red-and-white sticker for Rosington Football Club and a koala bear which wore a frilly apron.

Dougal frowned. *Who on earth—?*

As he opened the door, the sound of Sophie barking monotonously reached him through the partly open window of the kitchen. David and Benji replied in kind. It occurred to him that there was no point in trying to conceal his arrival; the engine and the dogs had already announced it.

On the other hand, Hanbury had already been attacked once this evening.

He jumped down from the car and ran into the coach-house. There was no time to pick and choose: he grabbed the gardening fork which stood just inside the door. He dashed back to the Range Rover and let out the Airedales. Once you had lost the element of surprise, you had to rely on strength of numbers.

The dogs bounded over to the back door, with Dougal just behind. The door was unlocked. Inside the kitchen, a single candle burned on the table. *When is James going to get the electricity fixed?* Sophie was by the door which led to the rest of the house. Her body quivered with rage as she barked; she was so absorbed in her anger that she ignored the new arrivals.

The dogs and Dougal surged into the hall in a compact, yapping cluster. It was in darkness but, as they entered, the sitting-room door was opened from within. Soft yellow light spilled out of the room beyond.

Hanbury was standing in the doorway. "What *are* you doing, William? Kevin and I—"

The Airedales had stopped short at the appearance of Hanbury, but Sophie charged grimly on. Her muscular little body was caught for an instant between Hanbury's leg and the door-jamb. Then, with a heave which sent Hanbury staggering, she was through into the sitting room. There was a crash of breaking glass. Dougal caught a glimpse of Sergeant Lewis trying to ward off the attack with a chair.

"For God's sake, William, can't you *do* something?"

Dougal propped his trident against the wall, hoping that Hanbury hadn't noticed this embarrassing encum-

179

brance, and went to rescue Lewis. Sophie had pinned the policeman in a corner; her jaws were locked around one of the legs of the chair; it was only a question of time before the tug of war ended in her favour. Dougal grabbed her by the collar and whispered vicious nothings in her ear. Lewis grasped the situation quickly and pushed against the chair.

The deciding factor was Dougal's grip on her collar. Sophie's strength, if not her will, diminished as she drew nearer to asphyxiation. She was gradually pulled and pushed across the floor to the door.

When she and the chair were safely in the hall, Dougal slammed the door and leant against it. Lewis, breathing heavily, said nothing until Hanbury had found him a fresh glass and poured him some more whisky. Hanbury was drinking as well, which was probably not the wisest thing to do after a head injury. Dougal himself refused: *Spécialité de L'Empereur* had left him with a furry tongue and a headache.

Lewis sat down heavily on the sofa and sipped his drink. "You should have that dog put down," he told Dougal. "It's a bloody menace."

"She's not mine," Dougal said firmly.

"But Jim said—"

Jim?

"Ah, no." Hanbury shrugged. "I wish she did belong to William. I misled you unintentionally, Kevin." He turned to Dougal. "I said you were the only person who had any influence over her." He sat down in the armchair. His bandage was a little askew, which had the curious effect of making him look forlorn and slightly ridiculous. "As a matter of fact, she used to belong to my wife."

There was an awkward silence. Dougal felt that the ghost of Molly Hanbury had become an intruder in her own house.

Hanbury stirred. "I don't know why she's taken so violently against you. Though I suppose she's fairly violent with most people."

"Nearly had my leg off when I tried to come in the back door. In the end I had to go round the front."

"I expect she took you for a burglar. Either that or she took exception to your colour scheme this evening. That jacket is really rather bright, you know."

Hanbury was right: the pattern on the tweed was a large check of olive green and mustard yellow; the blue shirt didn't help, either. Perhaps Lewis liked to be colourful in mufti, as a contrast to the drabness of the suit he wore on plain-clothes duty. But Hanbury's remark seemed gratuitously offensive—though Lewis had not taken it in that way. Then Dougal realized that the two older men were acting just as people did at an old school or college reunion: they were seeking the common ground between them, which in this case meant re-creating the pattern of their adolescent behaviour to one another.

Lewis drained his glass and held it out for a refill. "Don't talk crap. Everyone knows dogs are colour-blind."

Dogs are colour-blind . . .

"Are they really?" Hanbury splashed several inches into the glass. "So we're left with the burglar hypothesis. William, are you sure I can't interest you in a drink?"

Dougal shook his head. *Dogs are colour-blind—or, rather, monochromatic . . .* "I'd better go and feed the dogs. The Airedales must be starving."

He left the room, preventing by a narrow margin the re-entry of Sophie, and took the dogs to the kitchen. Sophie's fury abated dramatically at the prospect of a second supper. While Dougal opened the tins, the three dogs frisked round his legs and those of the kitchen table.

Occam's Razor—the fewest possible hypotheses. If one makes one absurd assumption right at the start, all the facts slot together, and the motives are obvious. But surely—?

Sophie barked, reminding him that he was standing there with the tins open and the bowls before him. Dougal spooned out the brown mass of gelatin, gristle and meat. Usually the sight of it made him feel faintly sick; this evening he didn't even notice it.

He put down the bowls and slipped out of the kitchen, carrying the candle from the table. Instead of going back to the sitting room, he opened the door on the other side of the hall. Dank air swept out of the study, making the candle flame flicker. Dougal went in and shut the door behind him.

He was alone in the room where Molly Hanbury had died.

Lewis took Dougal's return to the sitting room as the signal for his departure. There was some discussion in the hall about the manner of his going. In the end, the policeman left by the front door, to avoid meeting Sophie; he declined Dougal's offer to come out with him to his car.

"I'll see you tomorrow, Jim." By now there was a healthy-looking flush on Lewis's flat face. "Ta-ta."

Hanbury closed the door and locked it. He was paler than usual, but there was no mistaking the pleasure on his face.

"What was all that about?" Dougal asked. "Your mugging?"

"In a manner of speaking." Hanbury led the way back to the sitting room. "It's a straw in the wind, my dear William—another straw. If this goes on, I shall end up with an entire haystack."

Dougal sat down and lit a cigarette; he had stopped counting them several hours ago. Fatigue, worry and excitement combined to make him impatient with riddles. Something of what he felt must have showed on his face.

Hanbury took mercy on him. "My friend Vosper gets on very well with the local CID; I expect you've gathered that. He's obviously dropped a hint that I am to be included in the—ah—magic circle."

"So Lewis was just making a courtesy call?"

"I think he feels he may have been a little brusque this morning: making amends was part of his reason for calling. But he had heard about the mugging too—the station phoned the news up to the golf club. Kevin was having a drink with Claud, and old Claud was naturally very disturbed."

Dougal added the inflection of Hanbury's pronunciation of *naturally* to what he already knew of Vosper. "If you die suddenly, you've arranged for the publication of your dirty pictures?"

"Something like that. There are documents as well." Hanbury shrugged the subject away. "Claud's anxious for my continuing good health. Kevin was off-duty but he very kindly came along to see that I was all right. He reached the hospital soon after we left. He and his colleague will be making an official visit tomorrow, of course. But in cases like this they like to sort out the—ah—groundwork beforehand."

"Kid-glove treatment: you really have arrived." Dougal had a sudden and depressing vision of Rosington as a cluster of overlapping social networks. An individual's worth was measured solely by the number and quality of the networks to which he or she belonged. The thought jogged his memory: "I forgot to tell you; two more straws blew in this evening. Mrs. Palmer's coming back on Monday, as long as you get the wiring sorted out, and Mrs. Stride wants to ask you to dinner."

183

Hanbury raised his eyebrows; for an instant they vanished beneath the edge of his bandage. "I'm not sure that I'll accept. I'll have to think about it. By the way, did Leo say anything of interest?"

More than enough.

"He's desperate to recruit you to the anti-Pantry faction. I got the impression you could name your price." Dougal stubbed out his cigarette. "Look, James—"

He stopped of his own accord, unexpectedly overwhelmed by the prospect in front of him. A single question could usher in a host of consequences, though he had no means of telling which ones they would be. He shied away from assuming the responsibility. Problems were sometimes preferable to their solutions.

Hanbury's eyes were wary, even suspicious. "I haven't forgotten the reason why you're here," he said deliberately. "And I was—ah—surprised that you visited my father. I've got a splitting headache, and I feel like death warmed up. Even so, I think I'd like a progress report. Or an explanation."

Damn you. Dougal knew they were both tired and tense; he knew they should leave this until the morning. Old wounds bled more if you reopened them at night.

Yet he was also angry, because that was the only alternative to being scared. And anger made him say, "Do you remember me having tea with Pantry on Saturday afternoon?" *Lapsang Suchong and dead babies.*

Hanbury nodded. "But I fail to see—"

"It was something you said afterwards, or rather something you implied. It might tie up with two things I heard this evening." Dougal paused, as the potential consequences of asking a single question once more presented themselves to him. The only point in favour of going on with this was an obscure notion that the truth was somehow valuable for its own sake.

184

But who am I to play Nemesis in other people's lives?

"Does all this have any bearing on Molly's death?" Hanbury's voice was jerky, as if the words were being wrenched out of him by an outside agency. "If it does, I want to know about it."

It was an hour later, and the candles were guttering in their sockets. There were six candles in the sitting room, and each of them was flaring, hissing and dying according to some pattern of its own. Hanbury's face had become a battlefield on which light and darkness followed the fluctuating fortunes of war. The issue, Dougal thought, was never really in doubt.

Hanbury was talking about murder. "It's odd, isn't it? I've never killed anyone for what you might call an *emotional* reason, like love or hate. It always struck me as a rather unbalanced thing to do."

"It is." Dougal poured himself some more of the strong tea he had made. At his feet, Sophie whimpered in her sleep. "It won't solve anything. If we're right—and it's a big if—character assassination would be safer and probably a lot more effective."

"Difficult to prove anything—especially about Molly. No point in throwing mud if it won't stick." On someone forty years younger, the expression on Hanbury's face would have been a pout. "Are you sure of your facts?"

Dougal nodded. "I checked the encyclopaedia in the study while Lewis was here. But we haven't got many facts, just thirty-year-old hearsay and the hypothesis which fits it. A lawyer would laugh in our faces."

But Hanbury wasn't listening. "Trying to implicate me with that Gauloise butt on Plum Hill—do you remember? It's not just clumsy—it's bloody impudent."

"And desperate." Dougal drained his tea and stood up. "I'm going to bed."

The wick of one of the candles between them collapsed and drowned in its own molten wax. A wisp of oily smoke ascended like a soul to heaven.

"Desperate! Of course." Hanbury smiled unexpectedly. "There'll be another attempt to kill me, won't there? That'll solve everything. All we need do is to create the opportunity—and make sure we control the outcome."

Dougal picked up the tea tray. "So you want to stage-manage your own murder?"

"In a manner of speaking. Can you think of another way to put your hypothesis to the test? I can't."

Fifteen

"How nice of you to come and say goodbye to Grandpa."
Evelyn Pantry hopped back half a pace into his hall. "Won't
you come in for a cup of coffee before you go?"

"I only wish we had time," Hanbury said. "But William's got to catch the eleven thirty-two. You know what
the railways are like these days: the next train's after lunch,
and it's one of the slow ones."

"Parting is such sweet sorrow." Pantry peered over
his glasses at Dougal. "But only a temporary one, I hope.
I often think that Rosington casts a spell over people."

"You mean they keep coming back?" Dougal felt his
stomach lurch but managed to control his surprise. Pantry
talked so much that it was only to be expected he would
occasionally produce a remark which held an uncomfortable and unforeseen relevance for his listener.

Beneath the bandage, Hanbury's face was as bland as
ever. "Perhaps they come back for the people rather than
the place."

Pantry bowed, taking the compliment for himself. "Such
a comfort to know one isn't entirely useless," he murmured, laying a skinny hand on Dougal's arm. "And
when shall we see you again, dear boy?"

"In a few days." Dougal had to raise his voice, for Sophie was barking behind them in the Range Rover. "I'm borrowing Sophie to show her the bright lights."

"I'm *so* glad." Pantry gazed soulfully into Dougal's eyes. "So *very* glad."

Dougal backed away. "We must be off."

"Come to tea when you get back." Pantry waved at them as they climbed into the car.

Hanbury let out the clutch and the Range Rover rolled down the hill towards the station. "Well, that's sorted out. The news of your departure will be all over town by lunchtime."

"Is it really necessary for me to go?"

"We can't be too careful." Hanbury honked his horn and waved at Julia Westmoreland who was climbing slowly up the hill. "We've been through all this: there might be someone at the station or even on the same train. We have to create the illusion that I'm alone. Ring me about lunchtime, and with luck we'll be able to arrange the next stage. You'd better find a hotel, in case there's a delay."

Dougal glanced at Hanbury; he wondered if the older man was running a temperature. "With that head injury you should be in bed."

"All in good time." Hanbury pulled into the station car park. "Now—are you sure you've got the gun?"

There were two guns—Beretta Modello 1934s. Hanbury had cleaned them this morning on the kitchen table. Dougal, staring at these dismantled killing machines, had made a last plea for common sense.

"Why do you want me as your back-up? Why not Lewis? If we're right, and if Lewis is there—"

"I'm not having the police meddling in my private affairs." Hanbury, having reassembled one of the pistols, rammed home the seven-round box magazine. "You either give me your word that you'll help or—ah—I'll lock you and that bloody dog in the cellar until it's over." The arrogance drained away; Hanbury lowered the gun. "It's Molly, you see. That makes it personal."

Dougal had unwillingly agreed to help. The thought of himself and Sophie indefinitely trapped in the cellar was only part of the reason. There was also the inexplicable loyalty he felt towards Hanbury, his employer and even, though it was hard to admit this, his mentor.

But there was another, more powerful reason for helping. If he had been in Hanbury's shoes, and if Celia had been in Molly's—that would have made it equally "personal" for him.

Justice was not only blind: it was usually impersonal. The apparatus of the state was for the benefit of the state: it offered little consolation for a wronged individual. Hanbury wanted an older form of justice—riskier but, if it worked, far more satisfying.

And who was Dougal to deny him?

It was raining when Dougal and Sophie left the train at Cambridge; their departure came as something of a relief to the other passengers in their carriage.

As they walked along the glistening pavements, Dougal's thoughts moved restlessly among the events of the last few days and ranged uncertainly into the immediate future. He tested each link of his reasoning, looking—hoping—for flaws; but he found none.

The garage was further down the Trumpington Road than he had expected. The Ford Escort, which he had booked by phone this morning, was waiting for him. He found a room in a nearby bed-and-breakfast.

By then it was time to phone Hanbury: the call confirmed Dougal's reasoning and his fears. Their suspect had jumped at the prospect of a meeting with Hanbury, and had suggested a time and place where they were unlikely to be disturbed.

"Gave me a lot of flannel." Hanbury sounded unbearably cheerful. "Quite desperate. The exact words were: *We don't want to set tongues wagging, do we?* I said I couldn't agree more."

It took another five minutes to make the final arrangements, and then Dougal was left with eight hours to kill. He left the Escort in the Park Street multi-storey car park, with Sophie in the back and the Beretta in the boot.

The rest of the day passed in a daze; it was almost as if Dougal was a bystander on the fringes of his own life. He watched himself watching a Polish film at the Arts Cinema; there were illegible English sub-titles; it was set in Warsaw where it generally seemed to be raining, just like in the Fens. He ate two meals which he didn't want and denied himself the alcohol which he did. He returned to the car to feed and water Sophie; later he took her for a walk across Midsummer Common.

At some point he bought a picture postcard of his own college. He stamped it, wrote Celia's name and address in neat capitals and scribbled a brief note. He asked her to dinner, gave her the phone number of the Dower House and ended *All my love, William.* He dropped it in a pillar box before he had time to change his mind.

Perhaps the South of France wasn't such a bad idea after all.

It was nearly nine o'clock by the time he left Cambridge. He had twenty-five miles to cover, north-west across the Fens by minor roads. As dusk fell, the rain petered out. There was little traffic.

Sophie refused to remain in the back of the car; she wriggled through to the front passenger seat and lay sideways, with her nose rammed against Dougal's thigh. For once she was quiet.

The first sign of trouble came when Dougal was about five miles from his destination. The car acquired a tendency to swing into the verge. Dougal began to sweat. The steering grew worse. A minute later, the jolting confirmed his fears.

A puncture.

He glanced at his watch in the light given off by the instrument panel. It was a quarter to ten; he hoped to be in position in half an hour's time. At a guess he had about four miles to go.

If all went well, he could just do it.

But the misfortunes multiplied. The nearest village was three miles behind him, in the Cambridge direction. Around him was nothing but shades of darkness. No one else seemed to know of the road's existence.

He was forced to rely largely on his sense of touch. Loosening the wheelnuts presented the next problem; but they eventually gave way to persistence, brute force and bad temper. Dougal jacked up the car, swearing continuously as he did so, and went back to the boot for the spare wheel. When he dropped it on to the road, it landed with a dull, dispirited thud. The next problem had arrived.

The spare was flat.

In the end, he found he had lost twenty minutes and gained precisely nothing: there was no point in changing a flat for a flat. He had no alternative but to drive on, as fast as he dared, hoping that the wheel wouldn't burst into flames and that the steering and the suspension could stand the strain.

To make matters worse, Sophie found this method of progression so distasteful that she lost her torpor and began to bark. Dougal lost control of himself and shouted angrily at her. She took this as an invitation to take part in a trial of vocal strength.

At ten twenty-five, the headlights picked out the wall of Rosington School. Shortly afterwards, they came to the entrance to the back drive. The gates were open, as Hanbury had said they always were. Dougal turned in, and immediately swung sharp right. The jolting from the front nearside wheel changed in character as it rolled from tarmac to sodden mud.

Leaving the car there will be quite safe, Hanbury had said. *Only tradesmen use that drive.*

Dougal mentally added certain other categories of users to the list: murderers, victims, and their friends.

He drove cautiously over the rough grass and stopped the car on the shadow of the privet hedge which lined the drive. As he switched off the engine, the rain began to patter on the windscreen.

He was late.

When he opened the door, the next unforeseen event occurred. Sophie, intoxicated perhaps by the sudden draught of fresh damp air, scrambled over his legs and out of the car. Dougal made a grab for her collar as she passed; but he was too late; she wriggled under the open door and vanished into the bushes. Dougal swore silently and leapt out of the car in pursuit. A few seconds later, he realized the futility of this: it was dark; the undergrowth, once away from the paths, was the next best thing to impenetrable; and the only way to track Sophie was by the rustling she made, which was rapidly decreasing in volume and merging with the other sounds of the night.

At least she had stopped barking.

Dougal returned to the drive, abandoning Sophie. He ran uphill towards the school. The drive twisted and turned as he ascended. On either side it was protected from what Hanbury called the Wilderness, where Sophie was, by the high, thick privet hedge.

There was the roar of an engine on the road below. Its driver changed down.

Only tradesmen use that drive.

The engine, revving hard to cope with the hill, was drawing nearer. Dougal threw himself at the hedge. Its yielding, spiky surface repelled him. Light appeared, growing stronger every instant, round the bend he had just passed. Dougal flung himself down and rolled into the angle between the hedge and the drive. His right hand fumbled in his jacket for the gun.

The pocket was empty. The Beretta was still locked in the boot of the car.

Peter Carrot killed the engine and raised the visor. "What the hell are you doing?"

Dougal stood up, wiping his muddy hands on his trousers. "It sounded as if you were coming up very fast. I— I thought it would be safer—"

"Christ! You gave me a shock!! No one uses this drive in the holidays." Carrot clambered stiffly from his bike and walked a few steps up the hill towards Dougal. He was caught in the beam of his own headlight; his leathers sparkled with raindrops. In full-dress uniform, with the bike in the background, he became another person.

Everything was going horribly wrong. Faced with the squat, menacing figure of Peter Carrot, Dougal began to wonder if he had reached the wrong conclusion—and if he was not about to pay for it. Explaining Carrot's presence by coincidence was just too much to swallow. Perhaps medieval philosophy was not a reliable aid to detection after all.

A few feet away from Dougal, Carrot stopped and

unbuttoned one of his pockets. Dougal backed away, fearing the worst, and nerving himself for a sprint back down the hill. He would be out of the beam of the headlight, and it would take Carrot a few seconds to start the engine and swing round the bike.

But Carrot produced nothing more harmful than a packet of cigarettes. With unusual politeness, he offered it to Dougal, who shook his head. It took several tries before Carrot's lighter succeeded in producing a flame which could withstand the wind and the rain. He inhaled deeply, making a funnel of his hand to shield the cigarette.

"I thought you'd gone back to London," he said slowly. "Sally said she saw you down the station this morning."

Dougal shrugged. "I just went over to Cambridge for the day."

"But what are you doing here?"

"I was driving past the school, and Sophie wanted a leak." It was a weak story, but the best he could think of on the spur of the moment. "I let her out and she shot off into the Wilderness. *Sophie!*" Dougal yelled, to give colour to a story which at least held an element of truth. *"Here, girl!"*

"It'll be the rabbits. Thousands of the little buggers round here." Carrot paused; he was not a rapid thinker, but he got there in the end. "I didn't see your car."

"I left it at the bottom of the drive. The road's too narrow to park a car out there, especially"—Dougal added priggishly—"on a night like this. And what brings you over here?"

Carrot edged away, as if trying to distance himself from the question. Dougal waited, becoming aware of the rain penetrating his supposedly waterproof jacket and trying not to think of the passage of time. He had been late last night as well; but the penalty then had been no worse than a touch of social embarrassment. Tonight was different.

"He said I shouldn't tell anyone," Carrot muttered.

"Who did?"

"I don't know." Carrot dropped his cigarette to the ground, where it fizzled and died. "I got to be going."

"Wait. You owe me one, remember? Tell me why you've come here. I promise I won't pass it on."

"Screw that." Carrot turned to go.

Dougal hardened his heart. "The police still haven't found your mum's killer. Do you want me to tell them where you were on Monday night?"

"I thought you said they were after some French guy—"

"They haven't found him yet. They'll still be very interested in you." Dougal pushed aside the thought that the end never justified the means. "And it wouldn't rest on my word alone. That voice you heard wasn't a dream. I know who it belonged to."

"You *bastard*." Carrot turned back; with his head lowered and his arms dangling, he looked uncomfortably like a gorilla meditating a charge.

"Look, I need to know," Dougal said in what he hoped was a firm yet gentle voice; it sounded merely quavering to him. "I don't want to drop you in the shit. Just do me a favour. And yourself."

Carrot's defiance crumpled. "I don't know who it was. This bloke rang the flat from a call box this evening— must have been about six o'clock. He said—oh well, you won't believe this."

"Try me."

"He said if I rode across Big Side at ten forty-five, stopped outside the chapel and sounded my horn, I'd— I'd learn something about my father."

A warped desire to laugh, blended with panic, shot through Dougal. Their suspect had made a bizarre and desperate move which was nevertheless neatly designed to appeal to Carrot's childlike and obsessive nature.

"What did Sally say to all this?" he said.

"She wasn't there, was she? She always goes over to her mum's on Thursday nights. Besides, the bloke said I wasn't to tell anyone."

"You sure it was a bloke?"

"I think so." Carrot paused, groping for words. "The voice sounded sort of muffled, and a long way away."

"Go home," Dougal said with sudden violence. "For God's sake, go home and stay there."

It took two precious minutes to persuade Carrot to agree; and Dougal wasn't proud of the methods he used. As he cajoled, he considered the possibility of hitching a ride with Carrot—either to the bottom of the drive, to collect the Beretta, or all the way to Rosington Station and safety.

But the first alternative would take too long; and the second demanded a ruthlessness which Dougal did not possess. He felt a fleeting envy for the simple psychology of Buridan's Ass.

Carrot rolled silently down the hill alone; he had agreed not to start his engine until he reached the road. Somewhere in the Wilderness a dog barked twice; it might have been Sophie.

Dougal ran on—up the hill and towards the school.

Sixteen

The door of the staffroom was ajar. A wedge of light cut across the corridor. Dougal could see wet footsteps on the worn tiles. Voices murmured beyond the door; individual words were blurred by the pattering of the rain.

It was a good place for a meeting, Dougal thought. The staffroom window looked out on to the Wilderness and the back drive, where no one was likely to be at this time of night. In any case, the heavy curtains blocked out the light entirely. Few people stayed at the school over the summer holidays, and those who did lived around Big Side, a hundred yards away; it was unlikely that any of them would want to venture across the old classroom block and the quad, particularly in this weather.

He moved slowly up the corridor. At least there was no need to hurry now—the voices told him that Hanbury must still be alive. In the back of his mind, he registered the presence of the footprints, among them his own. Something would have to be done about those.

The conversation beyond the staffroom door sounded amicable. For an instant Dougal wondered if he was completely mistaken: perhaps this meeting should be taken at its face value.

Then he remembered the absence of a car in the quad and the implications of Peter Carrot's story. There was no easy way out: Hanbury was talking with a murderer.

The meeting had been arranged for ten-thirty. In the original plan, Dougal was to have been in the library by ten-fifteen, ready to intervene if needed.

His body had been reduced to a machine for making unwanted noises—the rustle of clothes, footfalls, the rasp of breath, and the thumping of his heart.

He reached the door. Nothing was visible through the crack except an expanse of blank carpet and the corner of an armchair. But from this position he could hear what was being said.

Hanbury was doing the talking; his voice was low and relaxed. " . . .I would advise you to think very carefully about that. You're looking at this the wrong way round: the truth is that *I've* set the trap and *you've* walked into it. I took the precaution of writing a letter which will be opened in the event of my death or disappearance. I enclosed a tape I made of our telephone conversation this morning. I know that doesn't constitute hard proof—but that's hardly necessary, is it? You've created a very successful illusion, but it won't stand up to close examination. It's like any conjuring trick when—"

A dog barked in the quad—imperious yaps which demanded attention.

Sophie.

From the staffroom came a thud, followed by the clatter of falling furniture. Someone in there was breathing heavily.

The door from the quad to the corridor—which Dougal had left unlatched as he had found it—was flung open to its full extent. Claws scrabbled on the tiles. Sophie cannoned into Dougal's legs. Having found him, she licked him with enthusiasm. Dougal automatically reached for

198

her collar. She was soaking wet and smeared with mud; she was also inexplicably pleased with herself.

Simultaneously, it seemed to him, the staffroom door opened and the corridor lights came on. Dougal found himself looking into the muzzle of Hanbury's Beretta, the twin of the one which he had left in the car.

The hand holding it belonged to Jonathan Stride.

"Dear God," Stride said. "Come in here and bring that dog with you."

Sophie tried to sniff Stride's shoes as he stepped backwards; she pulled Dougal, who was still attached to her collar, into the staffroom in her wake.

"Sit down over there." Stride nodded towards the inkstained table by the window. "Keep your hands where I can see them."

Dougal obeyed. As he crossed the room, he stared stupidly at Hanbury, who was lying on his side and breathing through his mouth in a series of ragged gasps. His bandage had been dislodged, either by the blow or by the fall, and the wound in his scalp was bleeding again. His face was grey.

Sophie licked the blood with uninhibited enjoyment, despite Dougal's attempts to drag her away. When he sat down, she lay on his foot and fell into a doze.

On the table was a heavy spanner, one end of which was bloodstained. Stride scooped it up with his free hand. It was easy enough to see what must have happened. Stride and Hanbury were probably sitting at the table, with Hanbury holding the gun. Sophie's bark must have distracted him—and the head injury would have slowed his reflexes. Stride must have had the spanner ready, perhaps concealed in the folds of his overcoat. Once Hanbury was on the floor, Stride would have dropped the spanner and gone for the gun.

Stride remained on his feet between the table and the

door. "So you're in this as well; I was afraid of that. Does anyone else know?"

"Not yet. But they will. James was telling the truth about that letter."

"It's such a bloody *pity*. I had it all arranged."

"Carrot lined up as the scapegoat?"

Stride stiffened. "What do you know about that?"

"I met him in the drive, and sent him home." Dougal wriggled in his chair: the foot beneath Sophie was going numb. "It was a risky idea, but it might have worked. Everyone would think that Carrot had finally gone over the edge. He's your son, isn't he?"

"Maybe. I hope not." Stride sounded as if he didn't much care, one way or the other. "Why on earth didn't you and James go to the police?"

"Partly because we had no proof—just a wild idea." Dougal's eyes strayed towards the gun. "Also—James hasn't much time for the due processes of the law. You're not the only shark in this particular ocean."

"He seemed so—so respectable. A typical Old Rosingtonian." Stride frowned. "How did you find out?"

"James asked me to look into Molly's death. A lot of the ill-feeling towards him seemed to stem back to the three of you and Alison. It occurred to me that James might have been the intended victim. Then I found out about Jermyn's murder. And then Alison was killed. It all pointed to you, except there was no conceivable motive."

Stride said softly: "What made you change your mind?"

"You made a mistake last night, in the cathedral. Westmoreland said cantoris, and you went to the decani side of the choir. Stride was an ex-chorister and it's hard to imagine him forgetting something as fundamental as that. At first I thought you might have misheard Westmoreland. But there was something else that didn't fit. James made a snide comment about your dress sense, just after

I met you. At the time I thought he was just being rude, but later it occurred to me that he might have meant you were colour-blind. And that tied in with Cumblesham saying that Stride had been turned down by the RAF because of his eyesight. But I knew *you* weren't colour-blind because of that business with the hassocks."

"But it might not have been red-green colour blindness—"

"It's by far the commonest form. Stride was very ashamed about it, but he told James one night when they were drunk. It's also incurable."

The bald head glistened with sweat beneath the powerful overhead light. "It would be very hard to prove that Jon was colour-blind."

"The Ministry of Defence might be able to help. They tend to hang on to files; perhaps they keep a record of why they turn people down." Dougal stopped short. For a moment he had forgotten why he was here and to whom he was talking.

"Go on. Where did you go from there?"

Sophie stirred in her sleep, and whimpered.

"If you weren't Jonathan Stride," Dougal continued, "you had to be Charles Jermyn. And the hypothesis made everything fit in—the murder at Pormon, the attempt on James's life, Alison's murder—right down to little things like you avoiding James's company, and Jermyn being a schoolboy actor with a talent for forgery."

"I *feel* like Jon. I've been him for longer than I was Charles Jermyn." Stride—as Dougal still thought of him—glanced at his hands. "I didn't mean to kill him, and I certainly didn't intend to take his identity. He came down to Pormon to—to taunt me. He was that sort of person."

"I know about the will," Dougal said gently.

"Something snapped. He was sitting there at the kitchen

table, laughing at me. And I grabbed his tie, at the back, and pulled—just to make him stop, I swear it."

Jermyn swayed on his feet, but the gun remained steady.

Dougal kept silent. He could visualize the scene with almost painful clarity: young Jermyn at rock bottom, realizing that there was one desperate course which might allow him to evade a murder rap and become rich. The risks had been horrendous, but in Jermyn's position even a forlorn hope was infinitely preferable to no hope at all.

"Jon was on a motor bike—he was due in Southampton that evening. I just took his place." The knuckles on the hand which grasped the spanner whitened. "I knew the Fleetwoods—my employers—weren't coming back for weeks . . . it was hot weather, almost like August . . . bodies decay. Physically, Jon and I were very similar. The passport was no problem. The photo was two or three years old. I grew a moustache on the voyage out. I needn't have bothered: no one in Sydney knew what I looked like. I did the best I could with fingerprints." He shivered. "Have you ever wrapped a dead man's hand around your toothbrush?"

That voyage on the *Pacifica* must have been a nightmare, nothing to do for weeks except wait for that hand on your shoulder: *Would you come this way, sir? The captain would like a word . . .*

"For God's sake!" Dougal's voice was far louder than he had expected. "Why didn't you stay in Australia? Why tempt fate and come back here?"

Stride's mouth twisted, as if he had a mouthful of bitter lemons. "You're too young to understand. I used to dream of England, night after night. Green fields and old grey buildings. Little roads and people with gentle voices." He shrugged. "I just wanted to come home." His eyes dropped down to the body on the floor. "Ask James: he knows."

He hadn't meant to settle in Rosington. He had driven up from London for the day, and ran into Pantry in the cathedral. Pantry had recognized him and accepted him as Stride. (After all, he cold hardly have been Jermyn.) Rosington society had been delighted to suck in a wealthy bachelor with impeccably local antecedents.

Old school ties, Dougal thought; nostalgia, seemingly the gentlest of emotions, had a grip like an octopus'.

"I thought I'd be safe," Stride continued. "Jon and I had been so close, we were practically the same person. The only risks were James and Ali. I got a private detective on to them. He dug up a notice of James's death in *The Times*; he couldn't find a death certificate, so I reckoned he must have died abroad." Stride shrugged. "It must have been another Hanbury. He traced Ali, though—and who she was married to. There didn't seem much chance that she'd come back to Rosington."

"I can understand why James was a risk; but why Alison? She can't have known you *that* well."

"She knew my skull."

"What?"

"There's a little triangle of bone that sticks out at the back of the skull. She found it that night in the cathedral, and we talked about it. Since I went bald, it's been completely visible."

Her arrival in Rosington had been a terrible blow to him. Since Molly had died, in place of Hanbury, everything seemed to be spiralling out of control. But it was not entirely unexpected—he knew of her husband's arrest. He calculated that the risk of killing Alison would to some extent be offset by the Paris connection which the police would be sure to uncover. When he phoned her, she had leapt at the idea of a nocturnal rendezvous on Plum Hill.

"I imagine blackmail was in her mind," Jermyn said

calmly. "Respectable married local politician in teenage sex and drugs scandal: you know the sort of thing. There were no flies on our Ali."

"And now what?" Dougal asked. "Do you mind if I smoke?"

"Yes, I do. Suppose I kill you both, and plant the bodies in the Wilderness. I walked here along the river; no one knows I'm in the school."

"James's letter and the tape will go to the authorities." Dougal pulled out his cigarettes and lit one. The gun wavered in Jermyn's hand. "The condemned man's last smoke—fair enough?" It was curious how lightheaded he felt. "If you kill us, you'll just make things worse."

He moved his foot again: it had gone to sleep. The slight alteration in Sophie's position caused her to begin snoring.

"Why worse?" Jermyn asked. "If I'm going to be accused of killing three people, a couple more won't make much difference. The point is, I've only got James's word that this letter has been sent. In his position—your position—it's the sort of thing you *would* say, isn't it? But there's a chance that you're bluffing. It seems to me that the best thing to do is to kill you and await developments. If the letter wasn't sent, I'll be okay; if it was, I can always disappear."

Dougal sucked hungrily at his cigarette. "Easier said than done. In this country it's hard to vanish for any length of time."

Jermyn bared his teeth in a grin. "It's not difficult if you've already got another identity. I made sure of that when I moved up to Rosington; I'm not stupid, you know. I do wish you wouldn't smoke."

"How did you do it?"

"The usual way: found a gravestone belonging to someone who was born around the same time as me. Got

204

hold of the birth certificate and went on from there. It's easy—I've got everything—passport, driving licence, you name it. I can slip out of Jon Stride and into someone else whenever I want."

Dougal believed him. It was easy enough to acquire a second identity, given time, money and attention to detail. Probably there was a rented flat or bedsitter, somewhere in London; Jermyn would pose as a travelling salesman, or something like that. If he had to use his bolthole permanently, no doubt he would shave off his beard; no one had seen Charles Jermyn's face in England for thirty years.

"So you see—it does make sense to kill you. I'm not going to throw all this away unless I'm sure I have to."

Hanbury's breathing was becoming more stertorous. His mouth was open, and he was dribbling. It was impossible to estimate how badly he was hurt. Jermyn was right, Dougal conceded—at least according to his own system of values, where the greatest good was to be "Jonathan Stride" of Rosington. If he killed them, he gained a slim chance of holding on to what he had, including that pink-and-silver ribbon around his neck.

Dougal's mind raced onwards. Jermyn was an amateur in some ways, for all his experience of killing. He should have searched both Dougal and Hanbury; he should have tied them up. It was Dougal's turn to gamble now. It all depended on two things: Jermyn's lack of experience and Hanbury's habitual caution.

"Look, I don't want to be sadistic about this." Jermyn might have been a schoolmaster with a cane in his hand: *This will hurt me, my boy, far more than it will hurt you.* "Perhaps you should close your eyes."

Dougal dropped his glowing cigarette butt on to Sophie's back, just below the collar; the table leg shielded the action from Jermyn.

"Just a moment," he said, casting wildly about his imagination for a delaying tactic. "You know that Cumblesham is beginning to suspect something?"

"What?" Jermyn looked puzzled, as well he might, but not suspicious.

A faint smell of burning hair wafted up to Dougal's nostrils.

"Your defection from the ORS meeting yesterday really upset him. He said—"

Sophie snarled. She got to her feet and shook herself; the cigarette rolled on to the carpet. In her simple mind, pain was usually connected with an external aggressor. Aggression could only be met with aggression. All she needed to discover was the source of the pain.

Her mysterious canine loyalty immediately ruled out Dougal. Even to Sophie's limited intelligence, Hanbury was obviously incapable of this unprovoked attack.

She growled, deep in her throat, at Charles Jermyn.

"Go for him, Oaf! Sic him!"

Dougal's voice was shrill and desperate. At he shouted, he scrambled to his feet. Sophie surged forward with astonishing speed, and leapt for the arm which held the spanner. Her jaws closed on Jermyn's wrist.

Jermyn gave an inhuman howl of pain, as he tried to shake her off. He levelled the Beretta at Dougal; his finger tightened on the trigger.

Pins and needles stabbed into Dougal's right foot, which Sophie had used until recently as a pillow. His leg gave way beneath him, and he stumbled sideways.

But there was no shot.

Hanbury had left the safety catch on; and Jermyn hadn't remembered to push it off. The gamble had paid off.

As Dougal regained his balance, he saw that Jermyn was using the butt of the pistol as a hammer on Sophie's skull. The fox terrier grunted as the blows landed, but she held on. Jermyn's screams escalated rapidly in volume and pitch. Blood dripped on to the carpet; it was impossible to tell whether it belonged to the man or the dog. Sophie's legs kicked in mid-air as she was swung to and fro; it looked as if she was having a fit.

Dougal threw himself across the room towards Jermyn. For an instant his anger, fear and calculation telescoped into a single thought: *this man is trying to kill my dog.* He drove his shoulder against Jermyn's side and pushed with all his might.

Jermyn, made top-heavy by Sophie's weight, tripped over Hanbury's body and fell heavily to the floor. Dougal stamped on the hand which held the gun; something cracked; he bent down and pulled the weapon from Jermyn's nerveless fingers. He backed away, fumbling for the safety catch.

"Let her go," he croaked, aware as he spoke of the absurdity of what he was saying. "Let her *go.*"

Jermyn's screams subsided into moans. He rolled on to his back, trying to touch his bloody wrist with his shattered hand. Sophie stayed where she had fallen, with the spanner beneath her.

But she was no longer Sophie: she had been reduced to her constituent parts—mud, blood, flesh, dog-hair and splinters of bone. But one of the parts was missing for ever.

"You bastard," Dougal said. "You've killed her."

He levelled the gun at Jermyn, who took no notice whatsoever. The Beretta was notoriously inaccurate, as pistols went; but that would hardly matter at this range. *The simple solution: it punishes the guilty, purges anger and satisfies justice, whatever that is.*

Hanbury cleared his throat. The tip of his tongue emerged and licked his dry lips. He swallowed, and his eyes flicked open. They were bright blue, with bloodshot whites, and they stared directly at Dougal.

"William," he said petulantly, "stop playing with that bloody gun."

Fug the scob!

The lore of Rosington School, as disseminated by Mr. Pantry, proved unexpectedly useful. The staffroom, like the classrooms, contained a fug-box, the waste-paper container which was like a large wooden cube without a lid. It was a long time since Jermyn had been forced to sit in one, and his posterior had expanded in the interim. He tried to protest, but Dougal was in no mood to be trifled with. Jermyn eventually managed to get himself in; his knees drooped over the edge.

Dougal ripped off his prisoner's OR tie and used it to bind his hands behind him, ignoring the squeals of pain.

Hanbury had slipped back into unconsciousness almost immediately. Dougal tried to make him as comfortable as possible on the floor, using cushions from the armchairs; but neither his breathing nor his colour was reassuring.

"I'm a rich man," Jermyn said. "Surely we can talk this over like reasonable people and—"

"Shut up." Dougal took off Hanbury's tie and used it to gag his prisoner. He found a pink-and-white scarf on the hooks by the door and bound Stride's feet for good measure.

Tiredness and shock had turned Dougal into a machine. He felt neither sorrow nor anger as he stripped off his sodden jacket and laid it on the carpet. Sophie's body was surprisingly heavy; he manoeuvered it, as gently as possible, on to the makeshift shroud.

Jermyn's eyes followed him round the room. Dougal ignored him: there were more important things to think about.

He tied the arms of the jacket across Sophie's body, to

208

hold the shroud together. He needed both arms to lift the bundle. At the door, he used his shoulder to turn out the light. A strangled grunt emerged from the back of Jermyn's throat.

It was still raining. Streams of water coursed down either side of the drive. Before he was halfway down the hill, Dougal's shirt and trousers were saturated.

The Escort was where he had left it, with the driver's door hanging open. The seat was wet, and there was a puddle beneath the steering column. Dougal put Sophie in the boot.

Reversing the car on to the drive was unexpectedly difficult: the wheels revolved, spraying mud along the side of the car, but they refused to grip on the soft ground. Dougal finally resolved the problem by using the mats from the car to give purchase to the three functioning tyres.

He drove slowly uphill and parked in the quad, as close to the door as possible. This was the difficult part: there was always a risk that someone might have heard the engine.

The scene in the staffroom was unchanged. Dougal bundled Hanbury into one of the armchairs which had castors, pushed him along the corridor and out into the quad. The movement brought Hanbury back to the fringes of consciousness, which made getting him into the back of the car easier than it would otherwise have been.

Hanbury slumped across the seat. "What's happening?"

"We had a puncture," Dougal said. "You bashed your head. I'm taking you to hospital. I'll be back in a moment."

Dougal wheeled the armchair back to the staffroom. He placed it in front of the fug-box, took the Beretta from his waistband and sat down. Jermyn's eyes widened.

"Listen," Dougal said. "I'm not going to kill you; it would cause too many problems. I'm not going to hand you over to the police, either." *Because that could be embarrassing for me and for James—respectable citizens aren't meant to carry guns.* "But you're finished in Rosington, and you're finished as Jon Stride. Understand? Understand? You've got another identity: use it. If you stay here, I promise you that one of two things will happen: either James will kill you because of what you did to Molly; or you'll be exposed as Charles Jermyn."

His captive nodded violently.

Dougal stood up. He found a biro in Jermyn's pocket and an agenda for the last ORS meeting on the table; the back of the agenda was blank. He untied Jermyn's hands. The right hand was swollen and obviously painful, but the fingers were still capable of moving. He laid the biro and the paper on Jermyn's lap. Finally, he pushed the chair out of the reach of those long arms, and sat down again. His hands were trembling; it was difficult to hold the pistol steady, so he rested it against the arm of the chair.

"Now," he said. "Let's tidy up the paperwork. We don't want to leave any loopholes, do we?" He lit a cigarette and succumbed to the childish temptation to blow smoke at Jermyn's face. "Just write at my dictation: 'I, comma, Charles Jermyn, comma . . . also known as Jonathan Stride, comma . . . confess that I strangled . . . my cousin, comma, Jonathan Stride, comma . . . at Pormon on the twenty-fourth of May . . .' "

Epilogue

STRIDE, Jonathan Richard—on August 3rd, suddenly in London. Funeral private.

"Well!" said Evelyn Pantry, tapping the announcement in *The Times*. "What do you make of that, duck?"

"Short and to the point, if nothing else." Hanbury lay back against his pillows. The room where he'd lived for the last few days was bright with flowers and flooded with sunshine; the hospital's private wing faced south. "Who put it in?"

"I suppose it must have been Clarence." Pantry cleaned the lenses of his glasses with a handkerchief of lilac silk. "Terribly difficult for him, poor chap. But Jon was his son-in-law, after all; and there's no one else to take care of all the arrangements. I wonder what will happen to Jon's money—I mean, Cynthia can hardly inherit it now."

"I still don't understand why she did it." Dougal, who was sitting on the other side of the bed, pulled out a cigarette but did not light it.

"Ring the bell, William," Hanbury said. "Nurse can bring us another ashtray."

"Jealousy: hell hath no fury like a woman scorned."

Pantry replaced his glasses and beamed at Dougal. "It's as simple as that. It was a late marriage, remember—she was besotted with Jon. That must have made the betrayal all the worse."

The nurse was the one who had been on duty in Casualty the previous week; she had mellowed considerably in the interim. The Hanbury charm, Dougal thought, was as effective as ever. She brought another ashtray and took the opportunity to smooth Hanbury's pillows.

"I don't know what I shall do without you," Hanbury said. "Perhaps I'd better not go home tomorrow after all."

"Really, Mr. Hanbury!" The nurse blushed and fled for the door. "You are a one!"

Dougal glanced surreptitiously at his watch: he had plenty of time before the train. "Had Mrs. Stride known about it for a long time?"

Pantry shook his head. "Derek Ainslie says not. But of course his information is second-hand—he's relying on what his colleagues in London tell him. It seems that Cynthia gave herself up to the police immediately afterwards. She said that she'd suspected for several months that her husband was having an affair—all those business trips were very suspicious, and perfume *does* cling, you know, however careful you are about washing. But it was only after he disappeared last week that she found the address. She found a receipted bill in the lining of one of his jackets. It was in the woman's name."

"Who was she?" Hanbury asked.

"Jon's paramour? Some young secretary—much younger than Jon. Between ourselves, I don't think she's terribly bright: Derek said she was all bosom and no brains. He set her up in that flat in Hendon eighteen months ago. (*So* convenient for the A1.) Told her he was a travelling salesman—can you credit it?" Pantry seemed more shocked by the fact that Stride had chosen to pose as a salesman than by the murder itself. "You could have knocked me down with a feather!"

"The papers didn't make it clear whether Cynthia was going to kill him from the first," Hanbury said. "Was it premeditated? Did she take the knife to Hendon with her?"

"Apparently not. She picked it up in the flat, on the spur of the moment. Jon answered the door, you see, and then his young lady came out of the bathroom to see who it was. Derek says she was wearing nothing but a towel."

"At least her defence can argue diminished responsibility. Perhaps she'll get off with manslaughter." Hanbury touched the plaster above his ear and winced. His face was unusually grim. "I wish to God we had a sensible legal system where you could argue *crime passionel*. If we were in France, the jury would probably acquit her. I'll have to make sure she gets a decent counsel."

Pantry glanced swiftly at Hanbury; the latter's vehemence had obviously aroused his curiosity. Then he turned to Dougal: "But we must count our blessings, mustn't we? At least it didn't happen in Rosington."

Dougal blinked. He could find no answer to this.

Pantry stood up. "I must be off—they're expecting me for tea at the Deanery." He held out his hand to Dougal. "Such a pity you have to leave us, dear boy. Are you going by train?"

Dougal nodded. "The four-thirty."

Pantry's handshake was closer to a stroke. "Well, make sure you come back soon." He released the hand and moved towards the door. "I'll see you on Sunday, James. Twelve-thirty for one. Oh, I should have mentioned: Sir George will be there."

"How nice," said Hanbury carefully. "I don't think I've seen him since the wedding."

"Our local MP. Charming fellow," Pantry explained in an aside to Dougal. "Now poor Jon is out of the running, we'll have to find someone else to take his place."

Hanbury appeared not to hear. "I do look forward to seeing him again. I've always felt his views are remarkably—ah—sound. It's really quite astonishing that he's not in the Cabinet."

Pantry paused in the doorway. "By the by, James, I don't suppose you've ever thought of adding Molly's surname to yours? It would look very well, wouldn't it—a sign of respect. Shame to see the old name die out. Just an old man's fancy, duck."

With a valedictory flash of his signet ring, Mr. Pantry was gone.

"Burnham-Hanbury," Hanbury said. "It has a nice ring to it."

Dougal grinned. "I thought Conservative candidates were chosen by Central Office."

"So they are. But they do take into account the advice of the retiring member, and the opinions of prominent local Conservatives. Of course, I'm probably far too inexperienced. On the other hand . . ."

On the other hand, Dougal thought, Hanbury would have the backing of Sir George, a well-respected County name, Pantry orchestrating the support of the school and the cathedral, Claud Vosper's assistance and—last but not least—an innate grasp of politics as practised by the school of Machiavelli.

He got to his feet. "I must be going, James. Mrs. Palmer's Wayne is looking after Benji and David. Don't let him dig up the rhododendrons, will you. I put Sophie there. Oh, and I'll leave the Morris at the station. Wayne'll pick it up tomorrow."

"Why not stay longer?"

Dougal shook his head. "Someone's meeting me off the train."

The image of Celia rose in his mind: she seemed infinitely desirable; she hadn't been to a public school; and she knew nothing of Rosington.

"William—tell me something before you go. If she was alive, would you take Sophie?"

Dougal shrugged. He said goodbye and left the room. As he walked down the corridor towards reception, the tiles beneath his feet seemed to ripple and blur. For an instant he had the odd fancy that the world around him was on the brink of dissolution.

In the car park, he thought of an epitaph for Sophie. It was adapted from St. John: *Greater love hath no dog.*

As the engine fired, he suddenly realized why he was so upset. He knew the answer to Hanbury's question: of course he wanted Sophie with him. The trouble was, *if* she *had* lived the answer might have been different.

The thought that he was crying for Sophie was so absurd that he began to laugh.

Perhaps Celia would understand.